China Thermonuclear Conflagration 2029

Worldwide Nuclear Winter

By

Thomas J. Yeggy

Copyright © 2025 China Thermonuclear Conflagration 2029: Worldwide Nuclear Winter by Thomas J. Yeggy

All rights reserved. No part of this book may be used or reproduced in any manner without written permission from the author, except for brief quotations in critical articles or reviews.

This book contains many historical facts, events, and scenarios, and care has been taken to ensure their accuracy. Even though some of the characters and events are actual people and real events in which they may have participated, this story is a fictional account of their words and actions and must not be mistaken for what they did or said during those events or might do in the future. The descriptions, dialogue, thoughts, and scenes are products of the author's imagination and how he perceived those events and people in his own mind and represent his opinion only. Finally, some events will take place in the future, those events and the participants are obviously fictional as none of them have happened yet.

ISBN: 979-8-9878884-8-3 Print version

ISBN:979-8-9878884-9-0 Electronic version

Authors Note

Many books have been written about the inevitability of this coming conflict. Most of them have been subject to criticism based on the unlikely narrative portrayed as the proximate catalyst for such a conflict. This book attempts to ameliorate critics' concerns about that aspect of such a conflict in two steps: climbing up the ladder one rung at a time until the only choice left is nuclear war, and by character development.

Geopolitical escalation dominance is a game of chicken played at the highest levels. The US and China ran out of rungs on that ladder in 2029. A nuclear war finally became the only course of action seemingly available to one side.

The portrayal of the action that takes place at various Missile Defense Agency locations is exciting and macabre at the same time. An attempt to blend asset capabilities, like the Aegis and THAAD—Terminal High Altitude Area Defense—system within this story was made. Ballistic Phase Intercepts(BPI) of Intercontinental Missiles (ICBM) must be made within three minutes of launch. Therefore placement of US assets capable of intercepting China's silo based missiles in northeast China must be located in a geographical area capable of accomplishing those intercepts.

An attempt to visualize the Chinese and Soviet positions on the issues affecting their countries' interests in keeping the peace was also made. With seven countries capable of initiating a nuclear war either intentionally or by accident, a depiction of such a war's effect on the atmosphere is explained in scientific detail. Given man's history and makeup such a war is entirely possible.

Unfortunately, humans have a history of resolving conflicts with wars that have left over a billion dead. It seems as if Freud and Plato's descriptions of a human's appetitive and id's basic urges are all too accurate in predicting the conflicts within the human soul that don't fit well within a system where there are minimal consequences for the exercising of those urges.

Table of Contents

Prologue 1
1 6
2 9
3 11
4 14
5 17
6 20
7 25
8 28
9 32
10 34
11 36
12 40
13 43
14 48
15 51
16 54
17 58
18 61
19 64
20 67
21 73

22	76
23	79
24	82
25'	85
26	88
27	91
28	93
29	95
30	97
31	99
32	101
33	103
34	105
35	107
36	111
37	114
38	116
39	120
40	125
41	129
42	131
43	135
44	141
45	145

46	148
47	155
48	158
49	161
50	163
51	166
52	168
53	171
54	173
55	177
56	181
Epilogue	186

Prologue

October 28, 2029, 0925 Hours
Situation Room, West Wing
The White House
Washington, DC

President Connor Armstrong looked at those assembled in the Situation Room at the White House. Twenty-five sets of wanting eyes stared back at him—some arrogant, others anxious—scrutinizing his every emotion. On one side of the table were uniformed officers, with enough brass and ribbons to accessorize an Easter parade. On the other side were the intellectuals Armstrong had populated his Cabinet with, adorned in the finest suits and dresses money could buy. But not every Cabinet member was present. Some were traveling. Others, well, who cared what the Agriculture Secretary was doing?

Less than five minutes ago, radar detected three inbound submarine launched ballistic missiles (SLBM) heading for Portland, San Francisco, and Los Angeles. The SLBM intercept status remained undetermined. All available staff had dashed to the Situation Room in the West Wing. Armstrong got there first, escorted by the military leaders who had been in conference with him in the Oval Office when he received the alarm.

Armstrong—the most photogenic President in US history, aside from John F. Kennedy—had run a campaign that fed off the nation's dissatisfaction with the previous administration. He'd won in a landslide election.

Tall, handsome, urbane, well-spoken, and a master of social media, the Californian possessed no governmental or diplomatic experience. His tan face, azure eyes, and dishwater-blond surfboard hair had mesmerized voters during the debates.

Armstrong was woefully unprepared for the responsibilities of his office. He gave his rehearsed look of all-knowing confidence to those around the table, but beneath the table, he rubbed his sweaty thumbs and fingers together, resisting the urge to wipe off the sweat on his pants.

He locked in his noble leader face, looked vainly around the room, and shouted one name—"*Rockton!* Where's Secretary Rockton?"

John Rockton pushed his way past the crowd at the door and took a seat. This Secretary of Defense and former chair of the Joint Chiefs of Staff was the only member of Armstrong's Cabinet who the Senate unanimously approved. One of the Senators, the cousin of Armstrong's opponent, said, "Pretty Boy's going to need at least one advisor who doesn't have his head up his ass."

Rockton was flanked by Saanvi Wali, the new Director of National Intelligence, and Ken Brighten, the National Security Advisor. Yuxuan Wu, the Deputy National Security Advisor and resident expert on Chinese weapons, was whispering in Brighten's ear.

Armstrong's Eisenhower-at-Normandy exterior may have fooled some, but Rockton knew better. He was sure Armstrong's stomach was doing the rumba and his throat was constricting.

Guy looks like he needs to change his shorts, Rockton thought.

Armstrong jumped right into the deep end. "Secretary Rockton, let's authenticate. If I remember protocol, we contact the Deputy Director of Operations for the National Military Command Center at the Pentagon."

Rockton looked over at the black briefcase. "Mr. President, give me the football. After we determine who the responsible party is, we'll pick a plan from the Black Book. Then, we need to assess the logistics of our assets with the Joint Chiefs and the U.S. Indo-Pacific Command. We will then decide what we want to accomplish. The National Security Administration and the Secretary of State will also weigh in."

Rockton paused to make sure he was not seeing Armstrong's glazed-over look of confusion and panic that he knew all too well. This was not a situation where anything could be left to chance. The President had become unusually quiet, a sign that he was considering the gravity of the situation rather than thinking of something to say to impress his staff.

Rockton continued. "We may not even want to use nuclear weapons. This isn't a major attack by one of the superpowers. It's three ICBMs launched from a sub. We don't even know if the warheads are conventional or nuclear."

Armstrong recoiled. "I'll be damned if I'm going to let someone fire ballistic missiles at the United States and not retaliate in kind." He saw the worried looks in the room and, like any good politician skilled at flip-flopping, added, "Of course, I agree we need to assess the situation further before we act."

Rockton knew he was back in control. "Thank you, Mr. President."

Armstrong resisted the urge to follow up with another response that would have further proved his total lack of familiarity with the nation's nuclear arsenal. Everyone in the room wished Vice President Hobart Chambers was in the Sit Room and that Armstrong was on the goodwill tour of Malaysia.

The President felt compelled to stand and say something he assumed would sound presidential. "When we find out who it is for sure, we need to make an example of them. Even if these ICBMs are conventional weapons, I want to bomb whoever launched them back to the Stone Age. Am I clear?"

Many in the room thought the President needed to be restrained before he started a nuclear war. Rockton had visions of the verbiage in the Twenty-Fifth Amendment dancing around in his head. Saanvi Wali could see that Rockton would need help controlling Armstrong's hegemonic reflex response.

Wali jumped in. "As Director of National Intelligence, I will share with all of you that our intelligence now indicates it was North Korea's 092 who fired the missiles. Additionally, Mr. President, communication intercepts confirm Kim Myong-sik, Admiral of the Korean People's Navy, has made many attempts to recall the submarine that launched the missiles. Our intercepts further show a rogue contingent of dissidents seized 092. Before we engage in any response, much less a nuclear one, I would advise restraint. I don't believe Kim Yo Jong is behind this."

Armstrong was well acquainted with Wali's acumen in the intelligence world and begrudgingly respected her opinion. At National Security Council—NSC—meetings where weapon system analysis and foreign relations affairs were on the agenda, Wali's position became Armstrong's policy.

Armstrong stared at Wali, but she didn't flinch even in the blaze of his blue-eyed glare. Sitting next to Wali, Brighten and Wu nodded their agreement to the let's find out before we nuke anyone concept.

Wu spoke up. "Mr. President, the National Security Agency believes that Wali, on behalf of the Office of the Director of National Intelligence, has a valid point. We can't pick a plan from the Black Book until nuclear weapons are called for and we know who we are attacking."

At just under six feet tall, fifty-seven-year-old Wali commanded the Situation Room. The JCS had come to respect her opinion on military tactics. Heads nodded on both sides of the table when she said, "I want us to monitor the situation as it develops on our feeds from the Missile Defense Integration and Operations Center in Colorado Springs. That is where we will find out if the warheads have been intercepted."

Everyone's attention turned back to the President. Having demonstrated what he considered the requisite bravado, Armstrong moved into presidential mode. "Okay, let's take a step back before we review the options in the Black Book. But I want everyone in this room to understand that the nuclear option *is* on the table. If we do not intercept these missiles, I'll be dammed if we're going to look weak in the face of a ballistic missile attack." He turned to his Chief of Staff, Sandra Simon. "Sandra, update the appropriate Congressional leadership."

Wali knew there was the potential for more attacks. "Mr. President, I advise that we adjourn to the Presidential Emergency Operations Center until we know if more missiles are on the way."

"Agreed. Let's go to the PEOC." Armstrong stood up.

Rockton didn't want to show up the Chief Executive, but he was concerned about Armstrong's notorious lack of organization. "Mr. President, where is the biscuit, sir?"

Armstrong fumbled through his pockets and then looked in his wallet.

"Here." His face lit with the pride of a six-year-old who had just washed his hands before supper.

Rockton made eye contact with Wali. She looked relieved. Armstrong had regularly been unable to produce the biscuit at National Security Council meetings.

Everyone scattered. On his way out the door, Brighten heard the President speak to no one in particular. "How the hell did we get here?"

1

1972

It was an interesting year, to say the least.

On February 1, 1972, Hewlett-Packard introduced HP-35, the world's first handheld scientific calculator.

On February 21, 1972, *Air Force One* landed in Beijing, China. Although President Richard Nixon had not been invited, he was determined to leave his diplomatic mark on the world.

In the early morning hours of June 17, 1972, five men broke into the Democratic National Committee—DNC—headquarters on the sixth floor of the Watergate Hotel in Washington, DC. Their arrests hit the news the following day. Most Americans shrugged. Everyone in the White House shuddered.

On September 5 and 6, 1972, Black September terrorists murdered eleven Israeli athletes at the Summer Olympics in Munich, West Germany, resurrecting memories of World War II atrocities.

The Dallas Cowboys won the Super Bowl on January 16, 1972.

MVP Wilt Chamberlain led the Lakers to their first NBA championship on May 7, 1972.

The Oakland A's made mustaches and white shoes all the rage when they took the World Series in October 1972.

And as the year drew to a close, the last *Apollo* moon mission concluded with little press coverage and even less public fanfare.

While each event in 1972 was significant in its own way, the most notable occurrence for Rasish and Chandra Wali happened on the first day of that year. On January 1, 1972, their daughter, Saanvi, was born in Cupertino, California. They had arrived in the United States five years earlier and were still steeped in the customs and traditions of their native India. Early on, it became apparent that their daughter possessed extraordinary mental capacity. But later, Saanvi's dreams of attending Caltech crashed and burned while she was eating breakfast on the morning of her sixteenth birthday.

"*Beti,*" her father said. "I have something to tell you."

Ever the polite child, Saanvi put her spoon down next to the bowl in front of her and looked at her father. "Yes, *Baba?*"

"Your mother and I have made plans for your future."

"Am I to go to university? I'm scheduled to graduate early, and with honors. Perhaps I can enroll in the summer." Earlier in the year, Saanvi had received a perfect score of sixteen hundred on the SAT—eight hundred in mathematics and eight hundred in evidence-based reading and writing. As a result, every Ivy League school was recruiting her, but she had decided on Caltech to study computer science.

"That would be lovely," her father said. "But you will not be attending Caltech. We have arranged for your marriage. The wedding is a week from today, on January eighth."

Most sixteen-year-old California girls, regardless of heritage, would have balked, protested, or run away from home. But Saanvi, as thoroughly Indian as she was American, nodded and finished her oatmeal. "Yes, *Baba.*"

Saanvi's intended husband, Kabir Patel, was five years older. People in his culture were beginning to speculate why such a good-looking, well-dressed young man had not yet taken a wife and fathered many children. He recognized the peril of imposing Old-World strictures on someone as obviously gifted as his teenage brideto-be. So, on their wedding night, he made promises to Saanvi—pledges he kept.

Saanvi gave birth to twin daughters, Advika and Bhavna, on November 17, 1988. In August 1992, when the girls were almost four, an age when they still required oversight but could bathe, dress, and feed themselves, Kabir announced to his horrified in-laws that Saanvi had enrolled at MIT and would be leaving for Boston in two weeks.

Oh yes, and the couple filed for divorce.

2

August 17, 1992
San Francisco International Airport

Kabir had steeled himself for the moment and was determined not to show any emotion. Neither he nor Saanvi had been particularly thrilled with the arranged marriage, but across the years, he had grown quite fond of her. She was intelligent, witty, and very pretty.

Saanvi loved the twins with fierce devotion, but although she was an attentive parent, she did not consider it her life's calling. She adored the girls, but deep in her heart, she took a sort of been-there-done-that approach to the whole motherhood vibe.

"I will do my very best." Kabir bit his lip. He could feel it starting to tremble.

"I'm sorry," Saanvi said. "But this is what I have to do."

"We're not going to argue again," he declared. "But you're only apologizing because it sounds right. You know you want this—you *need* this. And I'm at peace with that."

An announcement crackled over the airport speakers. "This is the final call for Flight 2711 to Boston. The door at Gate Thirty-One will close in five minutes."

"Don't forget the girls," Kabir hesitated. "And don't forget me."

He kissed her on the cheek. She would not see Kabir or her daughters for three years.

§§

It didn't take long for Saanvi to distinguish herself at MIT. Most students were put off by her aloof attitude and lack of social interaction. She regularly challenged her professors' conclusions and became quite smug until one day she picked the wrong fight.

"Ms. Wali, I'm sorry, but your coding solution is incorrect."

"No, it isn't, Professor Rutledge. You have made an error in your calculus, and I can prove it."

"Well, I think you should take a step back and review the solution presented by Mr. Hunter."

For forty-five minutes, Saanvi reviewed Bill Hunter's solution. She had been wrong. Most in the class felt like breaking out into a Bronx cheer, but sat there silently as the class ended.

Saanvi was walking slowly down the hallway when she heard a voice behind her. "Ms. Wali." She turned to find Bill Hunter strolling toward her. She just stared at him.

Bill broke the awkward silence. "I'd like to be friends."

Saanvi turned and continued walking. Bill stayed with her, doing all the talking. He was a couple years younger than Saanvi, but being a Robert Redford look-alike gave him quite a bit of confidence when it came to dealing with the opposite sex.

Finally, Saanvi broke her silence. "We can be academic friends, nothing more." Saanvi considered Bill her equal in intelligence, and he *was* attractive.

"Meet you at the library at seven tonight?" Bill challenged as he walked away.

Saanvi showed up at the library at precisely seven p.m., and Bill was already there. It took about a month for Saanvi to thaw out and let Bill be more than a friend. And Bill Hunter got what he'd always dreamed of—a beautiful woman with matching intelligence. They were inseparable for the next two years—but still academic competitors.

3

May 27, 1995
MIT, Building W16, Kreske Auditorium
48 Massachusetts Avenue
Cambridge, Massachusetts

Dr. Mildred Stransky called the students to order. "Good morning. As you know, we have a tie for the top spot in the graduating class. This morning, Saanvi Wali and Bill Hunter will be using identical hardware and software. Microsoft has supplied us with their yet-to-be-released Windows 95 and two of the latest Intel Pentium 133 MHz chips. Many of you are salivating right now because you know the chip has a CPU clock rate ranging from 60 MHz to 4.4 GHz and FSB speeds from 50 to 800 MT/s. For the literature majors in the group, that means it's very fast."

Everyone laughed, even the targets of the joke. The students in the School of Humanities, Arts, and Social Sciences were used to the ribbing—gentle and otherwise—from students and faculty members. Even with a non-science degree, a diploma from MIT would open all sorts of doors.

Dr. Stransky waited for the laughter to dissipate. "Saanvi and Bill will be given a problem to solve. They have not seen it, and to my knowledge, no one from the Delta House has stolen it from our offices."

The student body howled at the professor's *Animal House* reference. Stransky, though tough, was a campus favorite due to her devotion to her charges and her dedication to pop culture, even movies more than fifteen years old.

"As I said," she continued, "these two will be tasked with solving the problem using their own coding. The winner will be named valedictorian and will deliver an address at commencement." She fixed Bill with a withering gaze. "And it will be an…appropriate…PG address."

Once again, the hall dissolved into laughter. Bill Hunter was well-known for brilliance and bawdiness. His pranks were the stuff of legend, and his salty language had garnered more than a few official reprimands.

Dr. Stransky dimmed the lights and placed the problem on the overhead projector. It was a Carlitz-Wan conjecture problem. Stransky had obtained the answer from Hendrik Lenstra. She had convinced him to delay his publication until after MIT's commencement ceremonies. Bill solved the problem in three minutes.

The class roared with approval. Because the contestants were facing the audience, no one noticed that Saanvi had never typed a single line of code.

§§

Bill rolled over and rubbed Saanvi's back. "You threw the contest."

"Are you complaining about the way I just congratulated your triumph?"

"Not in the least. But my ego is not so fragile that I couldn't have handled losing."

"Well." Saanvi smiled. "You did everything you could to keep me in the hunt. If you'd taken any longer, people would have realized I was playing Tetris on my screen."

"Care to explain?"

"You helped me with coding my first year. For some reason, parts of it baffled me. Without your help, I never would have gotten a whiff of that silly contest."

"You're better than I am." Bill nodded. "You should have kicked my ass."

"Maybe so." She reached for him. "But right now, I have something much more pleasant in mind."

§§

Saanvi Wali graduated from MIT on June 4, 1995, just three years after she began. She moved back to the West Coast and, in a half-hearted attempt at reconciliation, joined her ex-husband in his fledgling startup in Santa Clara. They remained unmarried but got along well in the business. Saanvi homeschooled the twins, who had both welcomed her back with open arms. While she hadn't come home to visit in three years, she had never missed a weekly one-hour phone call with her children, even when it meant putting her studies aside.

One day, Saanvi heard a knock on the door of the small office space they had rented for Kabir's business. *Did I forget about an appointment?*

She walked to the door. "Who is it?"

No answer.

"Who are you with? Do you have an appointment?"

Apprehensive yet curious, Saanvi opened the door. A tall, wiry gentleman dressed in a conservative suit and out-of-date tie walked into the office.

"Ms. Saanvi Wali?" he asked.

Saanvi nodded and shook his extended hand. "I didn't catch your name."

"Probably because I never mentioned it," the man said. "Who I am is not important. I'm here to talk about your future." He reached into his jacket pocket, took out a leather folder, and showed her a badge.

4

June 16, 1985
Gulf Shores, Alabama

History has a way of differentiating between a visionary and a nutjob. It's called "the passage of time."

William Draper—Willy in the mid-1980s—always suspected his uncle was a little off. First, there was his uncle's name—Wilbur. The only person Willy knew with that name was the second Wright brother, and for reasons no one ever explained, the "other" flying bicycle repair shop owner was *always* listed second. Orville invariably came first, probably because he was sprawled in the middle of the wing when the *Dayton Flyer* floated off the sand at Kitty Hawk, North Carolina.

But the real tip-off to Uncle Wilbur's peculiarities lay in his obsession with "the coming trouble." At first, Willy didn't notice anything strange. After all, he only visited his uncle, his father's oldest brother, for a week in July every year when his parents went away together to "reconnect." When he was old enough to understand what they were doing on their trips, he was so grossed out that he begged to stretch his summer jaunts in the bayous of lower Alabama to three weeks.

His parents were only too willing to acquiesce.

Willy had just completed his elementary years when he decided, against all admonitions, to look in his uncle's basement. He yanked the cord that switched on the single 100-watt bulb hanging from the ceiling and gaped at the array of food and supplies. It took him a while to figure out why the room seemed so unusually large compared to the cabin above him. After a little investigation, he determined that someone—Uncle Wilbur, he assumed—had expanded the underground space far beyond the cabin's footprint.

Willy walked across the basement, through a gloomy, musty-smelling corridor, and into an expansive room. The walls were lined with more weapons than Willy could have ever imagined. He'd played with toy soldiers. He'd imagined himself as Wyatt Earp exchanging lead with the Clantons at the OK Corral. But never in his wildest dreams had he thought he might actually touch a Colt revolver or run his fingers along the stock of an M-16.

His reverie burst like a balloon when a deep voice resonated behind him.

"You can fire one of them if you want, Willy."

From that moment on, Uncle Wilbur taught young Willy Draper everything he knew about guns and survivalism.

"The Ruskies are gonna hit the moment they see a chance," Wilbur explained. "Everybody thought comrade Kosygin was an improvement over ol' Nikita, but I'm here to tell you, boy, none of those damn commies can be trusted. And I'm not all that crazy about the fancy-suited boys we have in Washington either. Kennedy was soft. Johnson wouldn't drop the hammer in 'Nam out of fear of the Chicoms. I hear a lot of talk about national defense, but I don't see any evidence of anyone stepping up to the plate to protect the ol' red, white, and blue."

Wilbur caressed an enormous handgun. "This is a .357 Magnum. It'll stop a charging rhino or take off a man's leg. Wanna hold it?"

"Is it loaded?" Willy hadn't felt such excitement since his friend Marcus offered to show him a copy of *Playboy* magazine purloined from a 7-Eleven.

Wilbur laughed. "Course it's loaded. Just don't get your finger anywhere near that trigger."

"Can we go outside and shoot it?"

"Not yet." Wilbur wagged his index finger back and forth. "At your size, the recoil would dislocate your shoulder." He looked at the disconsolate boy. "Tell you what. When you turn thirteen, we'll give it a go. Maybe you will have grown a little by then. But to make it up to you, let's go topside and shoot some cans with this .380. Just remember our deal. You never tell your folks *anything* about what goes on here."

§§

By the time Willy—now William—was old enough for the hand cannon, he was more than physically ready for what had become known as Dirty Harry's gun. At thirteen, he had grown to over six feet tall with thick legs and a solid torso destined to make him an all-conference defensive end one day at the University of Virginia.

William's summers with Uncle Wilbur came to an abrupt end when the eccentric gentleman died in his sleep after a generator malfunctioned and pumped carbon monoxide into his cabin. Seventeen-year-old William Draper was devastated.

The summer following William's senior year in high school, he packed his bags and headed to the University of Virginia in Charlottesville. The academic air crackled with the sparks of liberal thought, and Draper was exposed to progressive ideas and philosophy. Through careful consideration of the nation's history and a thorough examination of everything written by everyone from Thomas Payne and Thomas Jefferson to more contemporary thinkers, his politics moved ever farther to the left.

But he never forgot the lessons of survivalism he'd learned during his summertime trips to southern Alabama to stay with Uncle Wilbur.

5

November 10, 1994
Wiener Building, Room 104
University of Virginia
Charlottsville, Virginia

In high school, William Draper participated in the JROTC program. He liked it even though he was one of the few people of color. The order and discipline demanded of the men and women in the Armed Forces appealed to him, even if the right-leaning tendencies of the commanding officers and non-coms chafed him a little. By the time he was a senior, he looked damn good in a uniform.

Draper got a full athletic ride to the University of Virginia for his prowess on the gridiron. He also continued with the ROTC. When his junior year rolled around, the ROTC's commander summoned him to his office.

"Draper, you going to contract?" the lieutenant colonel asked.

"No, sir," William responded.

Surprise rolled across the commander's face. "You know you will likely be the top cadet by the time you're a senior next year, right?"

"Yes, sir."

"Are you dropping out of this program?"

"Not unless I have to, sir."

"Draper, you're smart, strong, and decisive. You're a great leader and the best cadet with a firearm I have ever seen. But you, son, are also a little strange. Obviously, you have a plan."

William did have a plan. If the NFL didn't come calling, he would matriculate to the Darden School of Business for an MBA and remain in the ROTC. As a show of thanks for the Army's latitude during his many years in the ROTC, William would postpone a business career and fulfill his ROTC commitment.

As a junior in college, William was a rising star on the Cavaliers' football team. The Wahoo faithful loved their Cavaliers, especially the ones who regularly brutalized the much-hated, blue-clad interlopers from Chapel Hill. In his first two seasons, William had already knocked three University of North Carolina Tar Heel quarterbacks out of commission with vicious but perfectly legal hits.

After Draper's senior year football season, the NFL passed him by. But he had been selected for an eight-week exchange program at the United States Military Academy in West Point, New York. He took an instant liking to one of the professors there—John Constantine—a visiting fellow from Gonzaga University in Spokane, Washington. Constantine was on loan to the Academy for a year as a lecturer in his field of legal expertise—philosophy and constitutional law.

Draper and Constantine struck up an almost immediate friendship—a mentor-mentee relationship. Their frequent discussions did not end when they both left the Academy. Both became fascinated and concerned about the rapidly expanding artificial intelligence industry and its impact on national security. They recognized after Deep Blue defeated Kasparov on May 3–11, 1997, in New York City, that machines were superior problem-solvers for extremely complex tasks with millions of variables.

They would stay in contact for the next half a century as they developed and carried out an intricate and—to many—frightening plan.

§§

The ink was barely dry on William Draper's MBA diploma when he walked into the U.S. Army recruiting office and signed his name. His original intent was a two-year stint. He stayed for ten.

Once he mustered out, Draper was inundated with job options. He decided on Webster and McAnally, a burgeoning private equity group. Five years later, McAnally's tragic and fatal skiing accident on a trip with his twenty-two-year-old mistress led to William Draper being promoted to managing partner. Twenty-four months later, weary of Webster's micromanaging, Draper opened his own business one mile outside of Webster's non-compete clause perimeter. Within three months, Draper's client list was lengthy and impressive.

By the time William Draper was forty, his name regularly appeared in *Forbes* magazine's list of the wealthiest individuals in America.

6

John Constantine

Some people grow up with a silver spoon in their mouths. John Constantine's parents would never have considered allowing their only child to be exposed to anything so pedestrian. Rhodium would have been more their style, but the price was exorbitant even for the Real Estate Wizard of Florida, as John's father Winston was known. Winston's wife, Judith, begrudgingly agreed to platinum flatware. They used the unengraved stuff for John's breakfast oatmeal.

Throughout his childhood, John was trained in the finest private schools. When he attended Yale, he became a member of Skull and Bones. Subsequently, he was one of the top graduates at Harvard Law School and then landed a PhD back at Yale in record time. At the age of twenty-seven, he was immediately in demand, even in a skinny job market. Offers poured in from every big firm on the East Coast. But with his financial security assured, John decided to teach. He took to it like bacon grease to fire.

John's family had always been wealthy. But in the teaching profession, no one suspected how much John was worth. He lived a conservative lifestyle, which matched his politics. He spread his wealth around so his name never appeared on any list. He drove a four-year-old car and eschewed expensive, European, attention-grabbing rides. After all, he lived in Spokane, where such extravagance would not mesh well with the citizenry.

John married a woman who most considered plain compared to the silicon-enhanced bimbos of his law school classmates who had jumped into jobs on Wall Street. While she was not the prettiest pastry on the shelf, she was brilliant and cunning. Either by luck or prescience, her parents had named her Minerva after the Greek goddess of wisdom and warfare. John had never met her intellectual or strategic equal. Together in partnership, they were as effective as they were ruthless.

Constantine and Draper were polar opposites. At six feet five, ebony-skinned William Draper was an imposing figure. Some referred to the diminutive John Constantine as "weasely." A notoriously demanding teacher, Professor Constantine leveraged his regular offers from other schools into a tenured position by the time he was thirty-four.

For years, Constantine's hair had been thinning. To avoid the look of a tonsured monk, he began slicking down his thinning hair from front to back. If it ever occurred to him that his hairstyle resembled Joseph Goebbels', he never mentioned it. Short and thin, he looked as if he might blow away in a heavy wind, but what he lacked in physical strength he made up for with an iron will and an expansive vision of the future.

Constantine took an immediate liking to his student William Draper, the hulking football star with a surprisingly quick mind. Constantine had always equated an intimidating physique with stupidity. But after he oversaw a discussion group at West Point about the state of US defenses and the threat posed by nuclear arms—a breakout session attended by fewer than a dozen mostly bored individuals—Constantine and Draper hit it off.

Constantine was genuinely impressed by Draper's questions and answers. Over the years that followed, Constantine would learn that Draper was working off the books as a consultant for the Central Intelligence Agency. He was tasked with identifying potential security threats, particularly those in the financial and cyber worlds.

Draper in turn did a deep dive on Constantine and his wealthy family. John's parents were large donors to every liberal cause imaginable, rivaling George Soros and Tom Steyer for prestige.

Draper found that the reason John Constantine broke right was the murder of Jessica Lunsford. He investigated the details of the murder and the fact that Constantine had led the charge in several states to enact "Jessica's Law" and determined that it was such a sensitive topic he couldn't bring it up with John.

§§

Constantine and Draper discovered they held different ideologies but shared similar ideas. They were both impressed with the fact that Plato and Freud agreed that human nature could be reduced to the same three elements.

Early on, the discussions were basic. Constantine didn't lecture Draper, but they did discuss how individual humans were the building blocks of any sovereign and that understanding human nature was critical.

"Okay," Draper opined. "Let's say that Freud's id and Plato's appetite are what give humans their primal urges. Let's say that Freud's ego and Plato's rational principle try to keep the id and appetite in check. What about the superego and the spirited parts?"

Constantine smiled and responded, "Ever done something you're ashamed of?"

"No!" Draper laughed.

"Well, that is your super-ego and spirited part whipping you for failing to control your id and appetite. Let's finish this with Hobbes' concept of the state of nature, where every man is for himself and there are no laws even against murder."

"That's crazy," Draper replied.

"Well, old Hobbesy was no dummy. He said to get the hell out of the state of nature and into a sovereign where you have some protections against the other guy's id and appetitive urges."

"What's the catch?" Draper asked.

"Have to give up some of those urges," Constantine explained.

"Not so difficult." Draper nodded. "I don't want to kill anyone unless they're trying to kill me."

"Well," Constantine added, "it's sometimes very complicated. Depending on how much security you want, you may have to give up many rights you think are basic. Then, even after you join a sovereign, they may be in a state of war with another sovereign."

"Head hurts. Stop, John."

Over time, Draper and Constantine both became disillusioned by current affairs and harbored a mutual distrust of all things governmental, especially the two-party system that they likened to the inbred royal families of Europe. The Great American Experiment had failed and was trapped in a never-ending cycle of self-preservation. The U.S. Congress and the Supreme Court have done little to nothing to end gun violence, health issues, and widespread corporate corruption.

Draper and Constantine had seen enough. They believed the entire system was spiraling toward the scrap heap of history where it would eventually join Alexander's Greece, Caesar's Rome, the British Empire of the eighteenth century, and Hitler's fascist regime.

They believed America's best and perhaps only hope lay in a broadly based, factually driven, readily accessible educational system. In their minds, the U.S. Constitution had inherent flaws. The monied ruling class—on both sides—was more interested in puppeteering than purity of motive. Having reviewed the writing of former Supreme Court Justices and Plato's *Republic,* they determined that the right to vote was superfluous. The idea was a considerable leap for the more liberal-minded Draper, but he had witnessed how politicians specialized in misleading minority voting blocs with glowing and consistently unfulfilled promises.

Constantine went over how and why democracies fail. His best example was the Hugo Chavez-Nicolas Maduro Venezuelan charade.

They could see the same pattern developing slowly in the United States. The two parties had become so polarized that the minute they wrested power from the other, the extremists in the elected party would point the FBI, CIA, IRS, NSA, and the courts at the head of the other party in an attempt to destroy them. It was a question of when and not if one or the other would be successful.

The two men began meeting regularly in secret. Despite their differences, their love of country and sense of what was best for America led them to formulate a plan. After years of talking negotiations between the two of them, they developed a framework.

7

June 12, 2026
Gonzaga University
Spokane, Washington

"We agree," John Constantine stated. "We're done with the primaries, the caucuses, the conventions, the massive spending."

"Yes!" William Draper pounded the table. Constantine jumped.

"Sorry," Draper said. "I'm just so damn tired of billions of dollars flowing through our system and buying favors."

Constantine smirked. "You've made that abundantly clear, but let's take it easy on the furniture. Nothing in my office is steel-reinforced."

Draper grinned. "Well, at least one of us is still in shape."

"Only one of us has *ever* been in shape," Constantine admitted. They both laughed. Their physical differences had long been a topic of genial ribbing.

Constantine continued. "Leaders will be determined through the educational process founded on Hobbesian, Kantian, and Platonic principles, slightly modified. We've got vestiges of the First, Sixth, Eighth, Thirteenth, and Nineteenth Amendments in here."

"Sounds good." Draper nodded. "We came too close on January 6, 2021, when QAnon, the Proud Boys, the Three Percenters, the Boogaloo Boys, the Oath Keepers, and NSC-131 stormed the Capitol, along with a bunch of clueless sheep."

"Didn't help that they were steered there by a narcissist who tried to wash his hands of the whole thing." Constantine bounced his bony hand on the tabletop.

"Easy there, big fella." Draper grinned widely despite the anger in his eyes. "We came damn close to a dictatorship. We need informed, educated leadership—not a collection of professional politicians whose only concern is holding onto their offices."

Constantine agreed and added, "Well, let's look at the Biden border policies. The Democrats, in the hope of getting millions more voters, opened the border with a wink and a nod to twelve to fifteen million people who would appear eight years later for an asylum hearing. The Democrats then used the court system to try to eliminate Trump. The Alvin Bragg convictions in New York were a farce and a mockery of justice. Don't think for a moment that the same wouldn't happen to every Democrat in Mississippi or Alabama if a DA brought charges. When that didn't work, they called him Hitler and a fascist, and then cut his Secret Service detail, resulting in two assassination attempts. Trump used every system imaginable—the FBI, the DOJ, and more—to return the favor. Is it hard to imagine that one of these times, one of the antagonists will become an autocratic regime?"

The friends went on to discuss every aspect of the wilting American culture.

No-bail systems that perpetuated violent crimes against its citizens by career criminals.

Widespread hunger in the wealthiest nation on the planet.

Children slaughtered in schools while intentional misapplication of the Second Amendment led advocates to offer the sole solution of "thoughts and prayers."

The rise of Internet "research" that continued to undermine decades of scientific breakthroughs.

Cities set ablaze by protestors who had abandoned the principles of passive resistance in favor of violence and destruction.

Tesla auto dealerships burned to the ground. People afraid to drive those cars because Elon Musk used his money to elect Trump in a move closer to an oligarchy.

Police officers held unaccountable when they exceeded their authority or ignored their training.

Elected officials more interested in padding their pockets than producing positive results for the very people who put them in office.

The plan continued to take shape. And years later, on October 28, 2029, when three missiles would break the surface of the ocean and head toward the continental United States, the nuclear genie would be released for the second time in history. Draper and Constantine would know that the time had arrived to, as Draper would put it, "put the ball in play."

8

October 5, 2003
5th Special Forces Group
Karshi-Khanabad (K2)
Uzbekistan Air Base

In 2003, twenty-six years before ICBMs would be launched at three West Coast cities, Edward McGonicle, the commander of the K2 Battalion, was responsible for controlling all US allied and ground forces in the theater. He was also charged with keeping Uzbekistan free of incursions from the Islamic Movement of Uzbekistan—IMU.

McGonicle shook his head. "The IMU is an awful bunch."

"So, I hear," Draper commented. "Some of the stories of what they've done to their fellow citizens are horrific."

"Cooperating with the Great Satan will get your eyes gouged out and your testicles crushed," McGonicle mused. "If that doesn't deter people from helping the US military, the IMU will come up with some really nasty stuff."

"What time is the briefing tomorrow?" Draper asked.

"At thirteen hundred hours," McGonicle replied.

"See you then."

"Not doing it." McGonicle shook his head. "Someone else drew the assignment."

"This guy got a name?" Draper asked.

"Saanvi Wali," McGonicle said. "*Ms.* Saanvi Wali."

§§

Draper tried not to stare at the woman giving the intelligence briefing. His attempts were failing. Saanvi Wali radiated both beauty and sexuality. Her army green sari did nothing to camouflage her feminine assets. Her walnut-colored eyes blazed with evangelical fervor.

Looks like a true believer. I hope to God she knows her stuff.

Saanvi knew how men saw her—an olive-skinned bimbo who must have slept her way to the top. But she also knew that once they abandoned their adolescent fantasies and began listening, they would appreciate the depth of her knowledge and the wisdom of her analysis.

Chief Master Sergeant Miller called the room to order. "Quiet!"

Even the officers stiffened. Everyone knew Miller. Everyone respected Miller. And everyone feared Miller. When he donned his dress uniform, his chest was so laden with ribbons and medals that Draper wondered how he managed to stand erect.

Then there was the distinctive five-point star hanging from a brass plaque declaring "Valor." Anyone who saw the award instantly recognized it as the Medal of Honor. Stories of Miller's exploits made Sergeant York's deeds sound like a preschool teacher rounding up a gaggle of rowdy toddlers. According to verifiable legend, Miller had taken out the last seven enemy combatants with his bare hands while bleeding from half a dozen gunshot wounds.

A jagged scar, courtesy of a Russian-made Smersh-5 fighting knife, ran from the base of his left ear to the corner of his mouth. When the Army offered to have the best plastic surgeon in the United States repair the wound, Miller responded, "Screw that. When can I get back to action?"

Miller nodded. "I'd like to introduce Officer Saanvi Wali of the CIA. She will conduct the briefing."

Murmurs rippled through the room.

Without asking permission, Miller stepped forward. "First asshole who whistles loses his trachea."

Even priests wished their sanctuaries were this quiet.

Saanvi Wali stepped to the front. She had long ago grown accustomed to stares and inappropriate whispered comments. "Thank you, Sergeant Miller. I appreciate your gallantry. But let me say on my own behalf, anyone who thinks they can take me, raise your hand. We'll go outside and see which one of us comes back intact."

The briefing tent erupted in applause. The men appreciated a woman with balls. Miller let the ruckus continue for fifteen seconds and then scowled. Order returned like a flash of summer lightning.

Saanvi nodded. "Like all your work, this mission is dangerous and complex. The IMU has kidnapped Lieutenant Nigel Wellington. Yes, he's several generations removed from the hero of Waterloo and therefore a British national icon. Imagine if someone abducted a direct descendant of Abraham Lincoln."

She let the comment sink in. "Our sources tell us he's being held in a hovel in Qarshi, about fifteen klicks from the landing zone. I'll give you some background, and then Colonel Draper will discuss the logistics. When it comes to tactics, I'm just another pretty face."

No one reacted until Miller chuckled. Then everyone in the room laughed and applauded—a nice moment of relief before yet another opportunity to stare the Angel of Death in the face.

Saanvi continued the briefing with an in-depth background of the IMU. Several key IMU leaders were reportedly associated with the abduction and assumed to be in the area. Taking them out would seriously cripple the organization. She knew the mind could absorb only what the rear end could endure, so she kept her remarks succinct. She took a step away from her position at the front, stopped, and then turned back to the crowd.

"You men and women are very brave, and this mission is of the utmost importance," She declared. "Watch your six and take care of your comrades. These are some very bad dudes—fanatics. They will not hesitate to pull the pin on a grenade and blow themselves up if it means killing even one American. This is my last comment, but I want you to hear this and take it to heart. The life of a foreign national, regardless of lineage or perceived importance, is not worth the life of a single member of the U.S. Armed Forces. Hooah!"

Every person in the room shouted "Hooah" at the top of their voices.

9

October 7, 2003
Uzbekistan

The Blackhawk careened through the sky fifty feet off the ground until it reached the designated spot. As soon as it touched down, Draper yelled, "Lock and load!"

Saanvi Wali had handpicked the Landing Zone based on intel from the NSA. It was an uninhabited valley nestled in the middle of rugged mountainous terrain.

The unit humped it until Draper held up a closed fist. He signaled four men to the right and four to the left. The remaining three followed him with the stealth of a leopard stalking dinner. Specialist Martin Schlegel silently crawled up to a low wall and took out two sentries with his KA-BAR knife. On Draper's signal, the assault began with John Denkman kicking in the front door of the building and spraying the first room with machine gun fire. The two men in the room died where they were sitting.

A guy called Hulk shattered the back door with his right foot. Draper had never heard anyone call the giant anything other than Hulk. Three more guards went down in a burst of automatic fire. A fourth shielded himself behind Wellington with a sinister-looking dagger to the Brit's throat. Draper put a bullet between the terrorist's eyes.

§§

"What's the 4-1-1 on the CIA chick?" Draper asked.

"I could tell you," McGonicle said. "But—"

"I know, I know," Draper interrupted. "You'd have to kill me." He tried to look pitiful. At his size, it didn't work.

"You constipated, Draper?" McGonicle asked. He didn't wait for an answer. "Hey! I gotta hit the latrine. Whatever you do, don't look at anything on my desk, especially the fourth file from the top."

By the time McGonicle returned, Draper was sitting across the room reading a magazine. But he knew everything in the fourth file from the top, everything there was to know about Saanvi Wali.

10

December 14, 2004
Prince Street, Apartment 204
Alexandria, Virginia

It had been nearly ten years since Saanvi Wali graduated from MIT. At her parents' behest, she had tried to reconcile with her ex-husband, Kabir Patel. "Think of the children, Saanvi," they had pleaded. But there were two major reasons the reconciliation didn't fly. The first sprang from the nature of any arranged marriage. Sometimes, despite the best intentions of parents and the pressure of cultural tradition, the couple just never meshes.

The second was Saanvi's continuing dalliance with Bill Hunter. They met as often as they could, despite the challenges of her training schedule and subsequent assignments all over the country and around the globe. Sometimes they managed to be together for several nights in a row. Other times, they went for long stretches without much contact.

On December 14, 2004, at seven p.m., Saanvi knocked on Bill's apartment door in Alexandria, Virginia, as planned. They had not seen each other for six months. When he didn't answer the door, Saanvi let herself in with the key he had given her. She gasped. The place was barren—not one piece of furniture, not one picture on the wall, no trace of anyone ever living there.

She walked out into the hall and knocked on a neighbor's door.

Mark Miller answered. "Hi, Saanvi." His congeniality faded like a sudden sunset. "Guess you're looking for Bill."

She nodded.

"Not sure how to tell you this," he said.

"Try," she encouraged.

"A couple of nights ago, two guys in suits led him away in cuffs. Yesterday, some dudes who looked like they might have done time emptied the place."

"What the hell?" Saanvi threw up her hands.

"I asked one of the movers where they were taking the stuff, and they said it would be in a storage facility called Keep It Secure. I went over there, but there was no record of anybody opening a space in the last two days. That's all I know," Mark explained.

Saanvi wasn't supposed to know about Bill's work, but he'd revealed things when they were in bed that she knew could get him in trouble.

"Thanks, Mark," Saanvi said. "I'll figure it out."

Mark was about to ask some questions, but Saanvi ignored him and turned to walk quickly to her car.

No matter where she searched, it was as if Bill Hunter, the esteemed MIT graduate, had never existed. Saanvi put it in the back of her mind and buried herself in her career.

Sometimes excellence matters even in government work. Saanvi enjoyed a meteoric rise through the ranks. She was named head of the CIA/NSA Joint Special Collection Service (SCS). Now she had access. She confirmed Bill Hunter's employment from his hiring date in June 1995, right after graduating from MIT, until he was "reassigned" to the Department of Defense in May 2004.

Then the trail went cold. *Odd. No digital trail even in our files.*

11

January 5, 2005
NSA Listening Station
Pine Gap, Australia

Saanvi Wali exited the NSA Listening Station in Pine Gap, Australia. She saw William Draper coming toward her, heading to the door. He was hard to miss. Saanvi waved and walked toward him.

"Draper," she smiled. "Good to see you again. This is a nice coincidence."

Draper feigned surprise. He'd come to the meeting specifically to see her. "Well, I didn't expect to find you here either. Figured you'd be leading the Agency by now. Got time to catch some coffee?"

"Sure," Saanvi smirked. "Just as soon as you tell me why you are really here. You're one lousy actor."

Draper laughed. "You've always been too sharp for me. Langley asked me to come down here to shepherd you around. Chinese kidnappers and the like."

"You don't usually do muscle work, Mr. Draper. I thought once you got out of the service, your gig was in the financial realm."

"True, but I'm a pretty good deterrent." Draper paused and flexed his right bicep. He liked to think he would have ripped his shirt if he had been wearing long sleeves.

"Had a lot of training outside your Army work, have you?" Saanvi couldn't help but smile.

"Since I'm not married, I've spent a lot of time learning other...uh...aspects of the craft."

"Like protection services?" she asked.

"Along with self-defense, a little surveillance, stuff like that." Draper purposely remained vague.

"So, you're not wearing your shirttail out because it's casual Friday?"

"Nope," he shook his head.

"What are you packing?"

"S&W 500."

Saanvi chuckled. "Why don't you just pull a howitzer behind you? Same stopping power."

"It's a little tough to tote around those 47-kilogram shells." He laughed.

"Can you sit down with that cannon in your waistband?"

"I opted for the four-inch barrel," he said. "I'm good." They began to walk. "You must have yours in your purse."

"Mark VII Desert Eagle," she said.

"Pretty stiff recoil on that bad boy."

"I'm stronger than I look." She flexed a little. "And my pistol's name is Petunia."

§§

January 5, 2005

Hotel Royal

Hsinchu, Taiwan

Twelve hours after Saanvi talked to William Draper, she was safely ensconced in her hotel room in Hsinchu, Taiwan. In another room, Draper slipped on a shoulder holster and a linen jacket, and then went down to the lobby for a threat assessment and to verify feasible escape routes should the situation warrant flight. He also strolled through the parking lot, looking like a disengaged tourist. But behind his wraparound shades, his eyes took in everything.

The hotel had added an oblong four-story high floor-to-cciling window addition in an attempt to compete with other more modern hotels like the Lakeshore Hotel in the East District, but the old fifteen-story main tower gave away its age. Still, Draper assumed the Agency had picked it because it was easier to secure than the newer hotels with twenty-story atriums that provided a sniper's nest for assassins.

He went back to the hotel, stepped into the elevator, and pushed eight. Just before the doors closed, two Asian men slipped in. Draper immediately noticed how deliberately they avoided making eye contact.

Rookies.

The second the doors shut and the elevator began moving, the men whirled, knives in hand. Draper dropped the one closer to him with a savage elbow to the temple. The man was dead before he hit the floor. His companion made a critical mistake. He glanced at his buddy, which gave Draper just the time he needed to drive the palm of his right hand into the attacker's nose. Stunned, the man dropped the knife and staggered backward. One long stride brought Draper within arm's length of the man. His pawlike hands grabbed the sides of the attacker's head and twisted. Draper grinned a little when he heard the dry-branch snap of cervical vertebrae breaking.

Draper stepped out onto the eighth floor, leaned back in, and pushed the button for the basement.

"Someone down there can take out the trash," he said out loud.

§§

Saanvi took one look at Draper's face and went back into her room for her bag. They were halfway down the hall when the fire door opened, and two men charged at them. Draper never broke stride. He snapped off two kill shots from his Sig Sauer P226. Draper hated wearing the thing because the suppressor made it feel like he had a tennis racquet under his jacket. He was glad the primary noise in the hall was the sound of the enemy agents hitting the floor like bags of wet sand.

In the garage, Draper and Saanvi met the last two members of the death squad. Draper hit the one on the right with a .40-caliber pop to the chest, followed by a shot to the head. He turned to help Saanvi, only to see her pulling out a stiletto from the other attacker's throat.

"Ready to go?" she asked.

"Yep," Draper nodded. He jumped when she touched the bloody spot on his jacket sleeve.

"You okay?" she asked.

"Yeah," he said. "But now I'm pissed."

"First time you've been hit?"

"No, But I really like this jacket," he smirked.

12

September 18, 2020
Nvidia Headquarters
Santa Clara, California

Draper had spent the last ten years travelling up and down the west coast meeting with venture capital companies looking for the next best iteration in the Artificial Intelligence world. He was a competitive chess player, and ever since Deep Blue beat Kasparov in 1997, he was all in on AI. During that decade, he had stayed close to Saanvi and her family. He caught up with Kabir late on a Friday afternoon in the late summer of 2020.

"Mr. Patel. William Draper from Vishay Capital Group is here for his two o'clock appointment."

Kabir Patel pressed the intercom button. "Thank you, Elaine. Put him in conference room six."

Draper looked at everything in the room while he waited. He'd never seen such an impressive array of displays and screens with graphic interfaces. Kabir entered the room.

He's done well. Designer suit, tailored, thousand-dollar haircut, Brioni shoes complete with slight lifts.

The men shook hands.

"Colonel Draper," Patel acknowledge. "I've heard a lot about you. Saanvi is very impressed."

I wonder if he knows I saved her life. And if she told him how enthusiastically she expressed her appreciation later in the evening.

"Please call me William," Draper said. "Your former spouse is a remarkable woman. Very accomplished in—"

Patel interrupted. "You can drop the charade, Colonel. We both know what she does for a living. Saanvi and I may be divorced, but I know her very well. I was never fooled by the…uh…'training trips' she took back East. She's obviously working for the CIA, the NSA, or something more sinister. Never fear. I have not told and will not tell anyone what I know."

Draper forced a grin. "Well, at least that's what you suspect."

Patel did not return the weak smile. "What I *know,* Mr. Draper—William—is that this is all unnecessary banter. Let me show you what we have."

Patel ran through everything—GPUs, CUDAs, and a fledgling project called the Alex Net Neural Network. He finished with a flourish. "This is the future, Mr. Draper—machines outthinking and outperforming human beings, all for the benefit of the world."

Draper nodded appreciatively. "Very impressive. Saanvi said you were on the cutting edge. She undersold you."

"Thank you." Patel dismissed the techs who had assisted with the presentation and took a seat opposite Draper. "I understand you want to meet my daughters."

"They work at Google, correct?" Draper asked.

"Sadly, they're very Americanized. When they finished their doctoral work at Caltech, they decided it would be best not to work with family."

"I'm trying to learn everything I can about your field of endeavor," Draper confessed. "Do you mind if I meet with your daughters?"

"As I said, they're free, independent thinkers. The best way to guarantee your access to them would be for them to find out I had prohibited it."

Both men laughed.

"I appreciate your time," Draper said.

"You're most welcome." Draper was halfway out the door when he heard Patel laugh and say. "And watch out for Saanvi. She's as addictive as heroin."

Draper stopped and turned around. He smiled at Kabir and said, "I've had plenty of morphine, so I know what you are saying."

13

October 22, 2020
Starbucks
Mountain View, California

William Draper came away from his meeting with Kabir Patel convinced that, after sufficient data input, machines would be able to make better decisions than humans in many areas. Although he was unable to reach an agreement with Patel's CFO for a secondary offering, Draper began to devote more time to investigating all things AI.

Rain pecked away at pedestrians outside while Draper, Advika, and Bhavna sipped coffee in a Starbucks in Mountain View, California, near Google headquarters. At least Draper was having coffee. Whatever concoctions the twins ordered were too complex for him to follow and looked more like milkshakes than java.

Things sure have changed. Some of these baby-faced soldiers order this crap nowadays, but if a crusty old Sergeant Major caught 'em with it, they'd get left in the desert in an ammo bag.

"How's your mother?" he asked.

"You'd know better than we would," Advika said. "She's always skulking around some foreign country doing her James Bond shit."

Had Advika not smiled, the comment would have sounded bitter.

Bhavna wiped a little foam from her upper lip. "Mr. Draper, everyone in the family knows Mom is up to her neck in espionage. And my sis and I firmly believe you and our mother are a little more than business colleagues, but that is way too gross to discuss."

Both girls scrunched their noses and said, "Eww."

Draper laughed at their juvenile comment, and both girls knew that their charade had cleared the air on that subject.

From a professional standpoint, the young women valued Draper's acumen and appreciated his eagerness to assimilate new ideas. Over the years, Draper had become convinced that at some point, the last rung of the escalation ladder would be reached with China. He was intent on building facilities that went way beyond a bomb shelter in case he was right.

To get those system requirements right, he needed information from Advika and Bhavna. Then he called a meeting with Saanvi Wali's entire family.

§§

February 10, 2021
Starbucks 750 Castro St.
Mountain View, California

Kabir Patel, Saanvi Wali, and their twin daughters dropped their COVID-mandated masks down a bit and smiled at William Draper as they walked into the small bistro next to Google headquarters. Kabir shook Draper's hand. Saanvi gave him a socially appropriate hug. The young sisters demonstrated more enthusiasm and less restraint despite the stares from masked patrons still committed to California's social distancing order.

Despite Kabir and Saanvi's divorce in 1992, they had always maintained a pleasant, even friendly relationship. When Saanvi was in the area, she frequently dined with Kabir and his second wife. Kabir had married again in 2009. Draper always figured that Saanvi was relieved that Kabir had found someone.

"Thanks for coming," Draper said after an overly enthusiastic server had taken their drink orders—that included a double mocha cookie crumble for the twins. "I hope you got my emails about GPUs and data centers."

"We did," Kabir confirmed. "We didn't respond via email because of security concerns."

"Valid," Draper said.

"We've had a family discussion," Saanvi spoke up. "We have natural concerns about proprietary intellectual property. So, this is your chance to explain what you want to do."

Draper always appreciated Saanvi's direct method of communication, both in business and in more intimate situations. "I know you have concerns about an attack," he addressed. "Particularly from China. I'm in the process of planning a world-class bomb shelter—actually, more of a community. I need the latest iterations of AI preserved in the event of a conflict or aggression. I need to know the required specifications for an AI configuration, and I want your family to run it when the time comes."

Kabir ran his tongue across his teeth. "It's as I surmised from the cryptic nature of your communications, Colonel. You're a master of saying what you want to say without saying it."

"Guilty as charged," Draper smirked.

"Our daughters agree with us." Kabir slid a packet across the table. "These are the specs. As a starting point, the El Capitan 2-exaflop supercomputer is expected to consume thirty megawatts of power.

Draper looked frustrated. "English, please."

"Enough power for over five thousand homes," Kabir explained. "However, various factors could impact this figure should the worst-case scenario occur. The training phase requires more energy than the operations phase. Image inferences will have an energy usage up to 2.907 kWh per 1,000 queries. New processors will use even more energy. You'll need an off-grid power supply. Your best bet is West

Texas because you will not get the permits you need anywhere along the West Coast."

"Texans are all about the Benjamins, right?" Draper raised one eyebrow.

"No different from anyone else," Saanvi said. "Just not as heavily regulated."

Draper wanted to mention his Large Language Model. "I'm also interested in an LLM that would analyze facts of criminal and civil cases and take the place of a judge and a jury. The model would factor in the history of war and numerous political systems. I need solutions on how to govern a society, with an emphasis on the fairness found in the writings of a list of philosophers I would provide. It's an idea I'm pursuing—hypothetically."

No one at the table showed any signs of alarm. They knew Draper not only as a man of action but also a deep thinker. He was always tinkering with some idea or another. They'd long since quit trying to solve the Sphinxian nature of his political-philosophical mind. Draper always appreciated how they accepted his requests at face value.

Advika smiled. "You will need a lot of processing power to run such a system, at least as much as it would take to power a city the size of Barstow with a population of about twenty-five thousand. It will have flaws based on input. Why don't you send us a list of what you want in the database. The criminal and civil parts will be easy. Small claims models are up and running in Europe, and other research indicates AI models have been embraced when the system's reasoning shows that the parties' arguments were fully vetted."

Draper felt his pulse quicken but kept his face placid. "You'll get the information you need via email. If it's okay with you, I'll share your personal emails with Dr. John Constantine from Gonzaga University."

Bhavna smiled. "Colonel, we're pretty good about reading the tea leaves. Based on your previous emails, we've already completed an

LLM with everything you'll need. All you have to provide is processing power. We'll review Professor Constantine's list, but I doubt we've overlooked any mainstream philosophers or leaders. Mother told us about some of your ideas. They're all in the model. We haven't run any simulations, but the database is robust, and we're confident it covers everything you want. I'm sure we'll meet your expectations."

Draper didn't know whether to be thrilled with the answer or disappointed that Saanvi had shared their pillow talk. After all, she was in the spy business.

14

May 2022
20 Miles South of Marfa, Texas
30°24'61", N 103.68'97" W
Average Annual Wind Speed 9.4 MPH

Ron May, CEO of Underground Hardened Structures and Shelters, signed the contract. "Mr. Draper, this idea of yours is going to cost a small fortune. Are you sure about this?"

"Thank you." William Draper tried never to show emotion, but this time, he allowed himself a slight self-satisfied grin.

May continued. "The deep water well will be to your specifications. To be clear, you want an underground, one-million-gallon fuel storage tank. The shelter is to be ninety-six inches below the surface and 250,000 square feet."

"Correct," Draper responded.

Draper glanced at his TS-301 wind meter, which had consistently registered a steady wind speed of nine miles per hour when he walked the grounds with May. *Perfect for the wind farm*. May cleared his throat to get Draper's attention back.

" Ahem…Air vents and carbon purifiers along with reverse osmosis filters, right?" May asked.

"Correct."

"This is going to cost a bundle. It's the biggest contract we've ever had."

"Too much for you?" Draper asked.

Draper let a tight smile run across his face. "Not at all."

"Just wondering about the strain on your wallet." May grimaced. "You're spending a lot of money."

Draper tapped something on the desk. "That's a check for $150 million, Mr. May."

"You're not running drugs or something, are you?" May was only half-kidding, which he showed with a half-smile. "I don't want to get into anything illegal."

"I'm a hedge fund manager," Draper explained, obviously irritated. "The money is perfectly legit. It may not be as ethical as one would like with hedge funds taking fifty percent of clients' gains in the trillions of dollars, but my money is going to be put to good use."

May was visibly relieved. "Mind telling me what this is? Your plan has enough specialized water pipes to provide water to a small city."

"Not at all." Draper enjoyed talking about his mystifying project. "I want to make sure that when I do cryptocurrency mining, my facility is not disturbed, and the servers are properly cooled. Many of the mines have been subject to attack, so I want to fortify this compound so no one from the outside can get to me."

May looked properly chastened. "No offense intended."

"None taken."

"Well, I wish you luck, Mr. Draper. The project will take about three years."

"Does that include the twelve satellite shelters?"

"No, sir. Those will take another two years—and probably another fifty million," May winced.

"When we get within twenty million dollars, call me, and I will make things right," Draper promised. Draper had bought the surrounding sixteen hundred acres for his wind farm. May's electrical engineers had drawn up the plans, and Draper had forwarded them to all four members of Saanvi Wali's family for comments. The final plan had twenty-five turbines evenly spaced with 438-foot blades. Each four million dollar turbine would generate 1.75 to 2.5 MW, depending on the conditions. The feeder lines and main 230 kV transmission line were all buried and stabilized at a cost of thirty-five million dollars per mile for the main line. Draper added the largest magnetic generators and thousands of storage batteries to assure that the facility would never run out of power. The other parts of the facility had been carefully designed by Saanvi Wali and included food that would sustain five hundred people for twenty years. Draper and his team were ready. Just to be sure, he checked in with John Constantine.

15

September 22, 2023
Philosophy 101, Wolff Auditorium
Gonzaga University
Spokane, Washington

William Draper left the mind-body symposium early—boring as hell—and jetted to Spokane, Washington, to sit in on one of Professor John Constantine's classes. There were only a dozen students in the room. Even if Constantine hadn't known Draper for a very long time, it wouldn't have been hard to spot the former football star, and besides, the university had fewer than two percent African American students.

Constantine still employed the Socratic method in his teaching and took a certain sadistic glee in pounding the unprepared. His lectures included the history of human warfare back to archaic *Homo sapiens* eliminating Neanderthals 125,000 years ago. He painted a hopeless picture for humankind, pointing out that wars had accounted for about a billion deaths under various forms of government. Could any governmental structure control the slaughter?

Constantine peered at the student to Draper's right. "Mr. Eagleton, last week you agreed with Hobbes that if a person finds themselves in the state of nature, the only rational course of action is to join a sovereign. So, this week, you get to choose a sovereign. If you were to join a sovereign, would you be willing to give up your constitutional rights under the Bill of Rights in exchange for your family's safety? Hobbes and Plato say a monarchy or aristocracy is superior to a democracy if the ruler has half a brain. So, tell me about what type of government you would choose and why."

Bradley Eagleton had his eye on a computer science major. Philosophy 101 represented a check mark on his humanities requirement.

"I would choose the monarchy, but with a caveat."

"Interesting choice, Mr. Eagleton. We'll get to your caveat in a minute. As you now understand, the government you have chosen will collapse into a timocracy if your philosopher-king class in the next generation is not identified at an early age and educated properly. Last week, if I remember correctly, we also covered the demise of a timocracy. Remember the Putin example. The paramilitary Federal Security Service—the FSB in Russia—came into power, and an emerging oligarchy was just a matter of time. An oligarchy, of course, devolves into a democracy when the populace wants a slice of the pie and overthrows the greedy rich. So, what's wrong with our democracy, Mr. Eagleton?"

Eagleton stood as was the class custom. Having been caught off guard earlier in the year, the young man was prepared. "Democracies have two problems at the extremis," he said. "Relatively speaking, they are a seizure of the power structure by politicians seeking to eliminate any opposition by whatever means necessary and demagoguing the opposition, resulting in ideological mobs who sway people like Hitler to kill minorities. Today we have a complete lack of law and order along our borders and in our major cities—smash and grabs, Oath Keepers, Proud Boys, police stations burning, too many individual freedoms for a sovereign to function. Need I go on?"

"Yes. Your caveat, please."

"My philosopher-king lineage doesn't have the problems found in Plato's *Republic*, which is a determining factor."

"Oh, and how did you solve that problem?" Professor Constantine asked.

"My PK is a bot, one I designed. So, it will be damned intelligent." He slammed his fist on the desk, snatched his backpack, and stormed out of the class. His shouting reverberated down the hall. "And all it needs to do is access more data," he shouted. "It doesn't worry about breeding habits and the education of your effin' philosopher kings."

The other members of the class sat stone-still in shocked silence.

Professor Constantine laughed. "I embarrassed him on the first day. I bet he's been rehearsing his little tirade all semester. Now—back to the question."

16

March 2026

For the past three years, William Draper had watched the geopolitical scene deteriorate, making him thankful he had started his project with Ron May when he did.

For half a decade, China and the United States had been engaged in a tit-for-tat game of escalation dominance through an increasing array of political gamesmanship, covert actions, and semi-unidentifiable proxy wars. Those activities, along with the everyday trouble in the Taiwan Strait, were pushing the two countries closer and closer to outright armed conflict.

The only good news lately for the United States was that the Russians had withdrawn their forces from Ukraine after NATO agreed to allow two thousand Russian observers to remain and monitor NATO activities to ensure there were no offensive nuclear weapons in Ukraine. NATO had also assured Putin that Ukraine would never be a member of NATO. Putin was given a small part of the Donbas region, largely because the brokered peace allowed him to save face in a war he was losing. He was grateful for the hand the US President had played in salvaging his oligarchy. Putin felt China could have done more to help Russia regain Ukraine, and the relationship grew frostier with each passing month.

Even though still a staunch public Beijing ally, the Russian strongman privately criticized Xi's transfer of an aging 092 submarine to North Korea in response to other US provocations around the globe. The US President made his disapproval clear to the world by asserting that the submarine should be treated as a Chinese craft. He continued his smear campaign, asserting that any missiles fired from that sub at the United States should be considered an act of Chinese aggression.

§§

April 2026
Bandar Abbas, Iran

The British-flagged tanker *Stena Impero* sailed southeast into the Gulf of Oman, flanked by two Chinese type 055 Renhai-class destroyers. The tanker sat low in the water.

The USS *New Mexico* (SSN-779), a Virginia-class submarine commanded by Captain Vincent Calhoun, received an alarm from the transponder on the hull of the *Stena Impero*. It had been attached there by Navy SEALs while the tanker was being filled in Bandar Abbas in Iran with oil bound for the teapot refineries in Shandong, a Chinese province.

The sub stayed out of range of the destroyers until the three ships reached the Arabian Sea. US attack submarines intentionally harassed the destroyers, a successful maneuver that delayed their arrival by thirty days and left many of the refineries dry. This was the first time the Chinese had sent their top-line destroyers as escorts for one lone tanker.

Commander Calhoun knew he had to take some chances to get the information the Navy wanted on the capabilities of the latest sonar on the Chinese Renhai destroyers. But the safety of his ship and crew came first.

The XO, Lieutenant Commander Norman Griggs, the resident expert on Chinese ships, called out from across the control room. "Captain, top speed thirty knots. The 055s feature hull-mounted sonar and employ variable depth and towed array sonars aft. If they engage at short range, they'll use two triple 324 mm torpedo launchers. For longer-range action, they have anti-sub missiles they can fire from

VLS tubes, as well as two anti-submarine helos—a Harbin Z-9 and a Z-20F."

"Recommendations?" Calhoun asked.

"Caution is warranted, sir," Griggs said. "Our ECMs will enable us to avoid torpedoes, but for the most part, we're better off if we avoid engaging their sonar for more than thirty seconds because of their other assets."

"Dummy torpedoes?"

"Acceptable risk from fifteen, sir."

Calhoun fired several dummy torpedoes at the destroyers. They responded by giving chase, but silent running kept the *New Mexico* safe from detection. The skippers of the destroyers became so frustrated that they decided to tolerate the occasionally terrifying thump of a dummy "fish." Similar harassment measures occurred anywhere the United States detected a tanker carrying Iranian oil. After a while, shipping merchants looked elsewhere for easier, less risky opportunities.

Tension between the United States and China continued to rise. In response, China increased its support of Iran's nuclear program. The decision to transfer the 092 submarine to North Korea escalated matters, even though China had promised Putin that the Chinese Navy would control the sub. The submarine, capable of firing missiles from a submerged position, represented a significant upgrade to North Korea's navy. Cyberattacks, interpreted by US experts as originating in Iran and China, contributed to the tension. The Chinese Ministry of State Security hacked into major US telecom carriers and carried out frequent electronic attacks on U.S. Treasury Department computers.

No one wanted war, least of all the Chinese, but the escalation ladder only had so many rungs. Huawei, ZTE Tech, Dahua, Hytera, and TikTok had been banned from conducting business in the United States. In October 2023, President Joe Biden banned most iterations of NVIDIA chip sales from Taiwan to China after the H-800 series.

These hopper chips had enabled DeepSeek R1 v3 to mimic Chat GPT-4 in January 2025. To incentivize Taiwan, the United States approved a shipment of cruise missiles capable of reaching Beijing to be a deterrent to an invasion.

Saanvi Wali had openly disapproved of the move. She shook her head violently. "The Taiwanese will try everything they can to mount nuclear warheads on those missiles. We're trying to put out a fire with gasoline."

But nobody listened, and the clock kept ticking.

17

September 18, 2026
NSC Meeting, Cabinet Room
The White House
Washington, DC

General Brad Fagan from CENTCOM was recounting the history of Iran's nuclear program and American efforts to halt the enrichment program.

"In July 2020," he began, "Israel surreptitiously supplied centrifuges that exploded at Natanz, Iran. In November 2020, the Mossad assassinated Iran's top scientist, Mohsen Fakhrizadeh, with an AI device operated from Israel. The next year in April, the Operation Olympic Games caused a blackout at the same facility and did sufficient damage to set the program back several years. However, as the International Atomic Energy Agency reported in the *Financial Times* on November 22, 2024, Iran developed 160 of the more advanced IR-6 centrifuges. They have enriched uranium well beyond the sixty percent level, possibly reaching as high as ninety percent. That's prima enough stuff for the production of a nuclear weapon. ODNI estimates they have enough enriched uranium to make as many as fifty nuclear bombs in the 100 kiloton range. Netanyahu thought he took out all the facilities in June last year and failed. Then we followed up with the B-2 and the GBU 30,0000 pound Bunker Busters only to find out that 900 pounds of 60% enriched uranium had been moved before the strikes.

Fagan looked around for questions. When no one flinched, he continued. "Currently, we believe China is enhancing Iranian missile range and accuracy by supplying sodium perchlorate. Iran is turning it into ammonium perchlorate, one of the main ingredients for solid propellant fuel used in long-range missiles. NATO knows the best Iranian long-range missile, the Sejil-3, has a range of 4,400 kilometers and can carry a 1,500 kilogram conventional warhead. It is a three-stage, solid-fueled missile. In addition, Chinese scientists have been handing over sufficient technology to put London, Paris, and even Moscow into play. If the Chinese have shared nuclear warhead reentry technology with Tehran, the calculus changes considerably. Unlike the Khorramshahr, which was a liquid-fueled missile and required several hours of preparation, the Sejil-3 stands ready to fire in a Launch on Warning—LOW—situation. Preliminary plans for an assault on the enrichment facilities have been distributed on a need-to-know basis."

A voice to his left asked, "Where is the Uranium?"

"Mossad reports that all the Uranium was moved to sites just outside the blast range of the GBU's then back into the facilities over the last year. To refresh. There were nine sites that were enriching uranium—Natanz, Anarak, Arak, Ardakan, Bonab, Bushehr, Chalus, Fordow, and Darkhovin. Fordow was tunneled into the Zagros Mountain range approximately 125 miles south of Tehran and fortified by 7.6 meters of concrete. Mossad believes 400 of the 900 pounds of highly enriched Uranium is located there. Any assault will have to be well-planned and will require hundreds of boots on the ground."

Under-Secretary of State Douglas Raleigh frowned "I can't believe we're even considering this. We could set off World War III. God only knows what the Chinese will do in Taiwan. General, you can't be serious. Even last year in May Iran made it plain that the attack would be considered to have originated in the US. Reuters reported as follows:

""Iran strongly warns against any adventurism by the Zionist regime of Israel and will decisively respond to any threat or unlawful act by this regime," Araqchi said in a letter addressed to United Nations Secretary-General Antonio Guterres.

Araqchi said Iran would view Washington as a "participant" in any such attack, and Tehran would have to adopt "special measures" to protect its nuclear sites and material if threats continued, and the International Atomic Energy Agency watchdog would be subsequently informed of such steps."

Do we really need another 911 on our hands?"

General Fagan shrugged. "Mr. Secretary, the President asked for a summary of the situation in Iran. Any intervention represents a massive undertaking. Last month, the Abraham Accords were ratified by Saudi Arabia, but sources tell me that the Saudis are the moving force behind disarming Iran. They don't want to stare at the business end of a nuke. Same with the Jordanians. Hell, even Putin is a little worried based on what he's doing in Chechnya, but you would know more about that than I do. Despite our best efforts, the Iranians still fund the Houthis in Yemen, Hezbollah in Lebanon, and Hamas in Gaza through their Chinese sponsors from Beijing." He paused. "If there aren't any more questions, I'm due back at the Pentagon."

The President waited until Fagan shut the door behind him. "Anyone here have a doubt about what needs to be done?"

§§

The President scheduled a meeting with the JCS and US Central Command. He wanted a final plan. There was no way he was going to give Iran a chance to set the world ablaze. The Chinese could decide to retaliate against Taiwan or other targets in the South China Sea, but he wanted a National Intelligence Briefing from the CIA's resident expert on China.

18

September 20, 2026
George Bush Center for Intelligence
McLean, Virginia

Director of Central Intelligence Benton Hostetler called his team on Indochina into the conference room. "Tillman, the President wants a briefing on China's reaction to a hypothetical attack on Iran's nuclear enrichment facilities."

Jim Tillman had spent years as the Deputy Chief of Mission in Guangzhou, but was really an Agency asset with multiple visits to Beijing. He headed a five-person team. Tillman stared across the table at Saanvi Wali, waiting for a signal. She nodded.

"Director, we anticipated your question—"

Hostetler slapped his forehead in mock horror. "What? A leak inside Langley?"

Tillman laughed. "Not this time, but we all believe that Saanvi Wali has the best handle on the current situation in China. She should write the Special National Intelligence Estimate and deliver it to the NSC."

New to the job, Hostetler wasn't sure who Saanvi Wali was, but Saanvi could read the room better than anyone and knew what his hesitation meant. "Director, I can handle this report. I've been spending quite a bit of time on SNIE on Chinese military capabilities in the AI field during my career."

Hostetler recovered nicely. "Ms. Wali, this report will require some artistry from you. Even though I wasn't sure who you were, I've read your file. This report is not something a computer can generate based on modeling probabilities. Xi and his seven dwarfs need to be handicapped for political goals. They won't like their main oil trading partner getting shelled from here to kingdom come. Am I clear?"

Saanvi resisted saying "Crystal" because it sounded trite. "Yes, sir. You want a report that has more hedges than an options house."

Hostetler grinned a little. "Precisely."

§§

September 24, 2026
Oval Office, The White House
Washington, DC

NSA Director George Williams was worried. "Mr. President, we have already had an economic war with China over tariffs and forcing the sale of TikTok and other companies we have banned. This Special National Intelligence Report from Saanvi Wali has more holes than my 1993 fishing skiff. Look at what it says on page twelve."

He adjusted his readers and cleared his throat to add some drama. Several people in the room rolled their eyes. Williams continued. "It says, 'Although it is unlikely, we can't rule out an attack on Taiwan or Israel.'"

He slapped the pages onto the table and resumed his demonstrative objection. "Well, that is reassuring. This would mean putting boots on the ground for the first time since our withdrawal from Afghanistan, and you know what a disaster that was. It contributed to your victory in the last election. We don't need the risk right now."

The President patted his thinning hair. "I won the election because the American people love me—at least the ones who have any sense." He turned to Fagan. "General, can this be done as CENTCOM has outlined in the plan I got yesterday?" He knew the General opposed the plan.

Fagan chewed on his lip for a moment. "Most likely, but only at considerable military risk and probably at a high political cost."

"There will likely be thousands of Iranian casualties, and we cannot rule out the chance that Americans will be harmed or killed," Fagan explained.

The President stood up and peered out onto the South Lawn in his best approximation of JFK's reflective stance during the Cuban Missile Crisis. He did not turn. "Gentlemen, I have come to a decision. I cannot allow the Iranians to explode a nuclear weapon. The reports we have are accurate. Enrichment has reached ninety percent despite or because of our sanctions. Just last week, the Chinese intentionally severed a fiber optic cable near Hong Kong and threw the worldwide banking system into a panic. We need to send a clear message. This operation is a go."

19

September 25, 2026
Cabinet Room, The White House
Washington, DC

General Kurten from Central Command confirmed the plan which was similar to 2025 but this time boots were on the ground The first phase would involve eight Virginia-class submarines, along with the British attack submarines *Astute*, *Ambush*, and *Artful,* firing over five hundred Tomahawk Block V missiles. The subs enhanced the element of surprise and were tasked with taking out all SAM sites and open IRG bases. The Sejil missile sites were the primary targets—top priority. The President didn't want France's Emmanuel Macron pitching a bitch about how the United States put France in danger.

The second phase called for clearing the skies of any remnants of the Iranian Air Force left behind by Israeli F-35s and US F-35Cs from the USS *Ronald Reagan* and the USS *Harry S. Truman.* The last part of the plan called for an assault by a hundred ground troops per site, brought in by V-22 Ospreys from amphibious carriers stationed within 450 miles of the targets, except for those north of Tehran. Those targets were to be attacked from bases in Iraq east of Kirkuk. The Ospreys would have 800-gallon fuel tanks occupying part of the cabin. All assets were moved into place by October 15. H-hour was 0300 on October 17, 2026.

§§

October 17, 2026, 0500 Hours
Natanz Facility, Iran

After the Tomahawk missile barrage took out nearby SAM sites, Israeli jets could be heard thundering overhead as Colonel Rick Poole and his special operations group from the Special Activities Center of the CIA jumped from their copters three miles south of the enrichment center.

Similar operations were underway at the eight other enrichment sites in Iran. Israeli F-35s and the F-35C planes from the USS *Ronald Reagan* in the Persian Gulf had cleared the airspace for the B-2s to deliver another fourteen of the 30,000-pound Massive Ordnance Penetrator—MOP bombs in an attack similar to the operation a year ago. The fighters had downed numerous F-4Es and Su-24MKs before the Iranian Air Force grounded all their jets. Poole waited for the earth-shattering explosion from the MOPs and then moved cautiously toward the facility with radiation detection equipment monitoring his every step.

"Go time," he ordered into his headset. "Radiation levels are low."

The Iranian Revolutionary Guard did not lie down. They poured heavy machine gun fire at Poole, but a trio of F-35Cs unleashed a hellish air-to-ground missile barrage, and the landscape lapsed into an eerie silence, broken only by the thrumming of helicopter blades. At the end of the operation, all the enhanced uranium was destroyed, but Poole's men had walked into an ambush. The choppers returned to base bearing the bodies of thirty-seven dead American soldiers. Other sites were not as cleverly defended, but the other missions also suffered casualties.

China's surreptitious efforts to arm Iran with a nuclear weapon had fallen short. The watch in the Sit Room stretched from 1900 hours until the wee hours of the morning. Sporadic firefights broke out throughout the region. The President, his VP, and the other assembled officials watched the US death toll inch past two hundred.

The American public was outraged. Worldwide condemnation was immediate. Chinese fighters began routine flybys within inches of South Korea's territorial limits. Choi Sang-mok, acting President and Prime Minister of South Korea, issued a scathing rebuke of "the West's unilateral and unprovoked act of aggression." But the U.S. Navy's expanded presence in the Pacific quieted all other retaliation.

Israel took out a couple hundred Iranian ballistic missiles with its Iron Dome defense featuring the new Tamir interceptors. Putin secretly called the President and thanked him.

Saanvi Wali took note of China's tact. She understood that the immediate problem had been resolved, but there were other concerning issues. The Chinese were still improving their weapons through AI applications of DeepSeek. One of the main questions yet to be answered was whether China's tech industry was acquiring NVIDIA's Blackwell chips through the gray market in Singapore. President Biden had prohibited such sales in 2022.

NVIDIA sales to companies based in Singapore had escalated following the ban. One of Saanvi Wali's assignments was monitoring Chinese tech and all improvements to it. She suspected that some of the latest iterations of AI products in China were produced with the help of the banned chips. She knew the Navy's greatest security concern was Chinese subs.

The main problem addressed by Chinese AI—as yet unsolved as far as Saanvi and the Navy knew—was that the People's Liberation Army-Navy (PLAN) had not figured out how to dampen the noise from its submarine propellers to less than 105 decibels. Consequently, Chinese ballistic subs were useless. If the PLAN could quiet down its boisterous subs, tracking issues would escalate exponentially.

Keeping NVIDIA chips from reaching China through the gray market or by any other means was a matter vital to US security. Another vexing problem with National Security kept Saanvi up at night. If war came with China, she knew that Iron Dome or no Iron Dome, the United States would be unable to stop all of China's ballistic missiles in the mid-course phase. She knew that the best time for an intercept would be within the first three minutes, commonly referred to as the ballistic phase. With China basing its silos in northeast China, the only realistic location was Mongolia, a gamble she was willing to take.

20

July 31, 2027, 0349 Hours
Mongolia Ballistic Intercepts
Oyu Tolgoi Mine
Khanbogd, Mongolia

The two copper miners from Dalanzadgad walked along the cavernous tunnel more than a thousand feet below the surface. The younger one turned his head. "You've been here since day one. Why is that section fenced off? Safety issue?"

"No," the veteran miner shook his head. "I've never been in there, but my supervisor said the company closed it. No profit. Not surprising. I hear the tunnel is fifty percent taller and twenty-five percent wider than average. Several elevators. Big investment."

"Really! Maybe I'll wander in there one day and look around."

"Wouldn't if I were you," the older man said. "Lots of stories—men who go in there and never come out. Someone told me the company once hired a search and rescue team. Came up empty-handed."

"Thanks for the warning," the younger man said. He twitched as if someone had walked on his grave, and the pair continued along the corridor.

§§

The Ömnögovi Province supported just over three million Mongolians. Revenue from the mining operations in the Gobi Desert accounted for thirty-four percent of the national GDP. Income from China continued to decline.

China had been subtly diminishing the Mongolian influence over the population of Inner Mongolia for decades by encouraging the Han Chinese to relocate there. Han Chinese men were paid substantial sums to marry and impregnate Uyghurs in the Xinjiang region of western China. In August 2020, the Inner Mongolian government made an announcement. Ninety percent of the schools would conduct classes in Mandarin only. Anti-Chinese sentiment, which had been simmering due to religious oppression and alleged political bribery, erupted.

A crackdown hardened the opposition and led to a resurgence of radical right-wing groups such as Tsagaan Khas, also called Dayar Mongol. They flourished in the far southern Ömnögovi Aimag. US policymakers who had been overtly courting Mongolia's top officials for many years due to its geostrategic location, saw an opportunity. China, apparently oblivious, continued to persecute six million Mongolians who attempted to flee Inner Mongolia over the next several years.

By the time the June 2024 Parliamentary elections rolled around, anti-Chinese sentiment was widespread. It propelled an anti-Beijing coalition headed by the center-right former Democratic Party President Battulga Khaltmaa to a stunning victory in the 2024 election, resulting in forty-seven of the seventy-six-seat State Great Khural being anti-Chinese.

Ever interested in expanding its international influence, the United States oiled its way into every crack. By 2023, there were several diplomatic overtures and numerous instances of minor military field exercises. The Chinese Ministry of State Security—MSS—should have been alerted to what America was doing in Mongolia, but the Chinese had more pressing concerns.

In 2026, China experienced a great recession when its real estate market imploded, much like America's did in 2007 and 2008. As a result, the yuan crumbled to a low of .106 against the dollar, and the United States found more lucrative trading markets for imports in South America. Research on artificial intelligence passed them by due to their constant battle with Taiwan, which produced the GPU chips designed by NVIDIA and were critical to AI iterations that developed learning. In addition, the private sector recognized the United States as an AI-friendly nation when President Armstrong's predecessor guided several companies to invest in what would become "The Golden Dome for America". As a by-product that project revolutionized the detection and treatment of many cancers. It also increased the speed and accuracy of Ballistic Phase Intercepts by changing the fuel in the second stage to a liquid component. The newest phenomenon for the US tech companies, three-dimensional quantum computing research, was almost non-existent in China. The Chinese had no knowledge of US advances since the country's industrial espionage had been significantly reduced under the previous hardline US administration.

On the diplomatic front, Khaltmaa had visited the American President and agreed on the use of the U.S. Overseas Private Investment Corporation to help address critical development challenges in Mongolia. More funds were slated for Mongolia as part of the Third Neighbor Trade Act. Foreign aid for humanitarian reasons was drastically reduced while foreign aid flourished for countries like Mongolia that surrounded China, where the United States could deploy missiles aimed at China's ICBMs.

Militarily, a minor strategic relationship with Mongolia had existed since 2004 when the first U.S.-Mongolia Bilateral Consultative Council meeting took place. Mongolia supported US efforts in Iraq and later in Afghanistan. Since 2012, Mongolia have been actively engaged in NATO's Science for Peace and Security Program, considered by many as a precursor to NATO membership. For the past dozen years, Mongolia and the Alaska National Guard, along with other US forces, have engaged in a joint military exercise called Khaan Quest.

Mongolian leadership was cautious. They were well aware of the old Henry Kissinger adage: "It may be dangerous to be America's enemy, but to be America's friend is fatal." Khaltmaa, who had not been allowed to seek a second term in 2021 due to a change in the Mongolian Constitution, found himself back in charge after the Constitution was altered in 2024.

Despite being elected to a six-year term in 2021, President Ukhnaagiin Khürelsükh resigned after the stunning rebuke of his Mongolian People's Party in the June 2024 Khural. Khürelsükh distrusted anti-Chinese sentiment. He suspected it would end badly for the Mongolian people. In his resignation speech, he blasted the right-wing Democratic Party.

The CIA saw an opening. With the approval of then-DCI Samantha Trimer, the Agency moved to get Aegis missiles close enough to the Chinese silos in northeast China to implement BPIs in Operation Whack-A-Mole (WAM). The operation was led by Saanvi Wali, Deputy Special Activities Director of the CIA's Chinese division.

There was a certain irony to WAM. Almost sixty years earlier, Operation Andyar had pushed the world to the brink of a nuclear holocaust, but perhaps it was only timing. The Soviet buildup in Cuba transpired over a matter of months. The US placement of SM-3 IIB ballistic phase interceptors and Lockheed Martin RQ-170 Sentinel drones took several years to complete. Wali had made several trips to Mongolia.

About once a month, Wali boarded a 737 and landed at the Ovoot Airport some 200 kilometers west of the Oyu Tolgoi mine, ostensibly as either part of a military exercise or a humanitarian aid package. From there, Mark 41 launchers and SM-3IIB interceptors traveled under tarps at night, just as the Soviets had done in Cuba. Upon arrival at the mine, they were lowered on one of five huge elevators into the cordoned-off section of the mine. There, they were assembled and placed on elevators for rapid deployment in a crisis.

Just like Kennedy, Xi Jinping never expected a little nation of three million to take such an enormous risk in his own backyard. But Khaltmaa was descended from a long line of warriors. Saanvi Wali had sold him on the concept by promising large sums for development. When the Chinese source of funds dried up, the money Xi needed to stay in power wasn't available, and he needed a bump from the Agency's "dark pool." For the CIA, it was a simple equation: rate x speed = distance.

After consulting General Anderson at the Missile Defense Agency's Command-and-Control Battle Management Communications Network (C2BMC) in Colorado Springs, Saanvi knew that the ABM program could not deal with all the ICBMs from China once they hit the mid-course phase. Knocking out as many as they could in the boost phase was critical.

The SM-3 Block IIB interceptors had been withdrawn from Poland and Romania under President Obama, and production was cancelled. It was a bad idea from the onset. Geographically, they had little chance of ever making a BPI there, even at 7.5 km/s and a 10g rate of acceleration. Putin had pushed Obama not to deploy the SM-3 IIB in Romania and Poland because the Russian strongman erroneously saw it as a BPI threat to the Russians' ICBMs.

Saanvi Wali had convinced DCIA Samantha Trimer that BPI was possible because the distance from Oyu to the Chinese DF-41 silo sites at Yumen, Hami, and Hanggi was under 650 kilometers. The projected flight of the missiles over the North Pole was also geographically favorable. Since the interceptor's boost phase was primarily vertical and the second stage had enhanced acceleration due to its liquid fuel component, even a west-to-east trajectory intercept could be accomplished in the ballistic or early ascent phase with a proper alert.

The main reason for the cancellation of the SM-3 Block IIB was that the initial booster stage was twenty-seven inches in diameter and propelled by liquids that were prohibited on Navy vessels. The SM-3 Block IIA was only twenty-one inches in diameter, featuring a solid-powered boost phase, and it fit the Navy's existing launchers. The CIA took on the SM-3 Block IIB project after the DOD scrapped it in 2013 because the Agency saw the possibilities of a BPI intercept from an advantageous staging area. It was also because Saanvi was able to prod the Navy into modifying a few launchers on Aegis ships that would serve some of the more sensitive areas of the world.

Saanvi also utilized off-the-books funding to employ a team of chemists from Raytheon, Northrop Grumman, and Lockheed Martin to develop a liquid propellant designed to support a twenty-one-inch-diameter booster. It not only enhanced performance but also fit into the VL-41 or VL-57 twenty-one-inch launchers and nearly matched the SM-3 II B's potential for BPIs.

Saanvi saw the opportunity she had been waiting for in Ömnögovi, Mongolia. She developed a platform to launch twenty-seven missiles from each of the five elevator shafts. The ODNI did not believe that all 260 of the Chinese silos contained ICBMs. Even if they did, the CIA knew the mine shaft missiles would play a significant part in the Missile Defense Agency's ABM multi-layered defense strategy, a plan primarily based on mid-course and terminal-phase intercepts before the Mongolian deployment. The WAM plan included launching RQ-170 drones ahead of the SM-3 Block IIB missiles, assigning them to areas where the Agency suspected DF-16Bs would launch DF-17 nuclear Hypersonic Glide Vehicles (HGVs). Spotting and taking out mobile DF-41 missile launching sites was also a high priority for the RQ-170s. There was more fallout for China in the AI area.

21

August 2027

The United States had invested heavily in artificial intelligence, and China made a critical mistake by deemphasizing crucial research in the area. Punishing capitalists such as Jack Ma meant China was shut out of the capital market system. That dealt a severe blow to the nation's R&D, which then became solely dependent on state-sponsored funds. Direct funding was not the problem, but financing for peripheral projects that developed AI and produced intelligence for military applications lagged.

In early 2025, High-Flyer, a Chinese hedge fund, released DeepSeek. The DeepSeek R1 model could not compete with Open AI's o1 model's subsequent iterations, despite its claims of a superior database and reduced utilization of computing power. On simple tasks, DeepSeek was phenomenal as an Open Source AI. But the US proprietary database and its upgrades overwhelmed DeepSeek in missile defense development.

Even when NVIDIA compensated for Biden's 2022–2023 ban by modifying H-20 and A-100 chips, China finally ran out of black market Blackwell chips in 2026 and fell hopelessly behind in AI military developments. Nevertheless, the Chinese government attempted to acquire access to gray market chips in Singapore, a move destined to cause problems.

US developers understood that the models had to be dynamic, not static. The base US models were placed in a reinforcement learning environment and rewarded for providing correct answers to complex coding, physics, or mathematical problems, where text-based responses known as "chains of thought" were developed. Inference or computing time to run through endless possibilities, overwhelmed systems that were not equipped with the highest caliber chips commensurate with the task at hand. In cases where the system requirements were met—adequate database, algorithms, powerful GPUs, and sufficient test time—the AI was not only likely to provide the correct answer but also to reflect on and learn from its mistakes.

The implosion by Vanke and the Chinese residential real estate market left the Chinese government in a situation where it had to spend on domestic rather than military research. The second Trump Administration saddled the Chinese economy with tariffs it couldn't afford. When Trump dumped Biden's climate change mandates, the Chinese state-sponsored solar, wind-power, EV, and turbine businesses overproduced for the decreased demand. China endured a great recession from 2026 to 2027, ending any chance to fund AI military development. On the other hand, the United States had been working on AI military applications since 2021.

By 2021, the Heron Company in the United States had produced a drone capable of beating American fighter pilots in simulated dogfights. By 2026, the drones were more than a match for Chinese air defenses. They were deployed in Mongolia and India, where China continued to have conventional border battles in the Gorga Area. The Chinese significantly upgraded their submersible ship ballistic nuclear—SSBN—boats from the 092 model. By 2027, they had produced two active 094s, four active 094As, and two 096 advanced class SSBNs featuring a 12,000 km JL-3 SLBM. China's SSBNs were all based at Sanya. They were very noisy compared to the deadly US pump-jet propulsor Virginia-class attack submarines running in silent mode.

The older 094s were so easy to track that they might as well have been beating a bass drum on their way through the depths. Even the newer 096 models produced over ninety-eight decibels, a deafening sound level in the world of silent submarines.

The U.S. Navy Fish-Hook Undersea Defense Line—a seamless network of hydrophones, sensors, and strategically positioned assets—stretched across coastal areas of Northern China through the Philippines, all the way to Indonesia. Not a single Chinese SSBN could reach the Pacific without a Virginia-class attack submarine as an undetected shadow. Chinese subs entering the Sea of Japan from the south were subject to detection and monitoring by the Japan Maritime Self-Defense Force's—JMSDF's—robust hydrophone arrays.

In addition, the Navy's latest ASW plane, the P-8A Poseidon, could lower hydrophones and a magnetic compass to a predetermined depth and connect by cable to a floating surface radio transmitter. The hydrophones converted acoustic energy from the water into a radio signal sent to aircraft computer processors for a kill shot when required. In short, the Chinese were wasting their money on SSBNs.

The plan had been to acquire NVIDIA chips through Singapore in the gray market. The Navy alerted the ODNI that a broker in Singapore was running an operation designed to enable the Chinese to reduce the noise on their submarine's propellers to below ninety-eight decibels, which would make tracking them difficult if not impossible.

Saanvi Wali had another road trip to take. This one was off the books.

22

August 26, 2027
Singapore

The leased G-5 made good time. Saanvi had made the arrangements herself. No one could possibly trace the jet back to the CIA. She and her companion looked like two Americans who were too stupid—or too vain—to fly on a commercial flight into Changi Airport.

Saanvi Wali and her contingent of SAC personnel from the Agency arrived in Singapore on a hot, rainy August day.

Percy Hawkins smiled. "You couldn't land us an assignment in the Caribbean, boss?"

"It's a little hard to figure out what the Chinese are doing from St. Thomas," Saanvi said. "But I'll keep your suggestion in mind."

Saanvi pulled up the collar of her raincoat, stepped into the spitting rain, and walked toward the taxi.

The taxi driver was with the Company, and the car had been swept, so Saanvi knew she could talk. "DeepSeek, China's primary AI model, is making progress. It continues to rival results in the United States from Google and Meta. Our guys are using the latest versions of NVIDIA's chip called the Rubin."

"Sounds like there's a chipmunk in the woodpile," Percy quipped.

Saanvi squinted. "Damn, you people from South Carolina say weird things. You mean 'something's rotten in Denmark'?"

"Yes, ma'am," Percy said. "Only it sounds less snobby." They both laughed.

"We'll cover everything once we get to Singapore. Just remember your cover," she reminded him.

"I'm a software engineer from Silicon Valley." Percy stopped grinning. "I know my job, boss."

"I know you do," Saanvi agreed. "But this is your first time over here. You don't want to make a false step. Eyes and ears everywhere. I mean *everywhere*."

"Where are we meeting the other guys?" Percy asked. He was careful not to say "the other members of our team."

"I believe they're at the Carlton," Saanvi said with intentional vagueness. "They said they'd be in touch once they got their plans finalized. You know how disorganized they can be."

Percy played along. "Those Caltechies can't get dressed without help."

§§

Two hours later, the group of CIA officers met in a secure room at the Crowne Plaza. Saanvi took the lead. "The Internal Security Department in Singapore cracked down on shipments of servers to Malaysia in early 2025 after NVIDIA's financial results for 2024 indicated a huge increase in sales to Singapore. The ISD arrested three people on charges of deliberately misrepresenting the final destination of US-manufactured servers. The ISD also announced it was probing NVIDIA's customers, Dell and Super Micro Computer, for potentially violating US export restrictions by shipping servers with NVIDIA chips from Singapore to Malaysia. Our asset inside the ISD has been working for the past year to identify how NVIDIA chips are making their way to China."

"There's that chipmunk thing again," Percy chuckled.

Saanvi looked at him but didn't smile.

Percy lowered his head and mumbled, "Sorry."

"This isn't anything to screw around with," Saanvi said. "Access to the NVIDIA chips will put China on an AI par with the United States, and shit will hit the fan—most likely a nuclear-powered one. Everybody clear?"

All heads nodded.

"Strong evidence suggests that the shipments in question came from a warehouse in Jurong, the southwestern part of Singapore's Western Province. Next Tuesday, a truck carrying over a hundred thousand Rubins will head over the Johor Causeway at 2000 hours for delivery to agents working for the Chinese Ministry of State Security. Per Naval Intelligence, the PLAN is close to lowering Chinese sub propeller noise to less than ninety-eight decibels, at which point our Virginia-class subs might as well be blindfolded."

"Are we worried about a first strike?" Percy asked.

"Damn right we are," Saanvi admitted. "Tensions between Beijing and DC have never been higher. We cannot let the shipment through. Team A will take up a position in Choa Chu Kang. Team B will be across the bridge in Johor Bahru. The intercept will take place on the causeway. Our extraction point is Punggol. We'll be picked up by an S351 DCS, a Dry Combat Submersible. Neither the Malaysian nor the Singaporean governments have any knowledge of our operation. The tactics and rules of engagement are in your folders. Any questions?"

Team B leader Darren Simpson looked up. "Yeah. Four members to a team, and we're supposed to disarm the drivers and toss the chips without firing a shot?"

"Yep."

"Then why will we have four FGM-148 Javelins and MK-17 SCARs in our weapons cache?"

Saanvi Wali could have been commenting on the weather. "We do what it takes. That is all."

23

August 29, 2027, 1949 hours
Jurong, Singapore

Darren Simpson's voice crackled through the earpiece. "We've got two deuce-and-a-half leaving the warehouse."

Saanvi responded. "Copy."

"Uh-oh."

"Say again."

"They've got company—an armed escort. I'm guessing it's from Chinese State Security. Third truck—open bed. Six, seven, total of eight with Type-85 submachine guns."

"You sure about the weapons?"

"Roger," Simpson affirmed. "Probably leftovers from twenty years ago."

"Chinese Army doesn't use those anymore," Saanvi remembered. "Lousy first shot accuracy."

"Well, that helps us a little."

"Don't get cocky," Saanvi reminded. "We should be okay, but our chances of doing this on the QT just went out the window."

Saanvi looked to her left. "Percy, initiate the plan."

Percy didn't hesitate. He keyed his mic. "Fire in the hole."

He depressed the detonator handle. Two hundred yards from the bridge, a small charge popped and set a car ablaze in the middle of the two-lane highway.

"No one from the security service will fall for this," he mumbled. "They'll know it's a trap."

"True, but they're not in the lead," Saanvi pointed out. "The guys driving the chips will stop. But if you've got Plan B, this would be the time to hit me with it."

Percy grimaced. "Fresh out."

"Okay," she said. "We need to get within fifty yards. Lock and load. Move out and make sure you're ready with that second charge."

"Yes, ma'am. That's good thinking."

"Hope for the best, plan for the worst."

The first two trucks stopped at the smoldering car. No one emerged. Apparently, the drivers were under instructions to wait for the guys in the back if anything weird happened.

Saanvi keyed her mic. "Steady. Wait for the heavy."

Four soldiers jumped out of the trailing truck before it came to a stop. Percy aimed his long gun. "Hold," Saanvi whispered. "I've got 'em. When that thing stops, blow it to hell."

The brakes on the trail vehicle had not stopped squeaking when Percy engaged the charge that Saanvi had buried in the road. The truck burst into flames. Anyone hoping to escape the inferno was blown to bits when Team B hit the truck with two javelins.

Saanvi stood and shot two of the dumbfounded soldiers in the head. Percy and his teammates dispatched the other pair.

The drivers offered no resistance. They were only too happy to unlock the backs of their trucks and flee along the road as instructed.

The teams unloaded the crates, took out the chips, and chucked them over the side of the bridge.

Percy spat into the rushing water below. "Process with those, you commie bastards."

24

October 23, 2029, 0200 Hours
Hijacking of the 092
Mayang-do Navy Shipyard and Submarine Base
North Korea

Territorial disputes between North and South Korea over the last three years resulted in no less than fifty vessels being sunk in the northern Yellow Sea and the Sea of Japan. The KPN—the Korean People's Navy—wanted a longer leash from Kim Yo Jong to conduct offensive operations against the South. But Kim Yo Jong clashed with the head of the KPN, Moon Song-gil, and was ready to retire him permanently. But he had another plan. He had developed a loyal following during his career under Kim Jong Un and summoned them for a mission. Many of them were radical rogues he knew he could count on to carry out his orders regardless of the consequences.

§§

The moment Moon Song-gil heard about the transfer of the submarine from China to his homeland of North Korea, he knew what he was going to do. The world situation did not frighten him. It disgusted him. No matter how loudly the weaklings in Pyongyang growled, no matter how many threats the impotent dictators uttered, ultimately everything in the world was under the thumb of either Russia or the United States. Neither master was worthy.

The moment had arrived. Song-gil looked over his crew of handpicked dissidents. Their scowls reflected the discontent he shared following his dismissal as Daejang of the People's Navy by Kim Myong-sik. All Song-gil had done was advocate the sinking of South

Korean ships inside what he considered territorial waters of the People's Republic.

"Comrades and patriots," Song-gil said. "We're here this morning not only to take back our fishing rights and enforce our claims in the Northern Limit Line but also to reclaim the dignity of our Navy. We are going to seize the 092 and take it beyond the sonobuoys. I have no illusions about the future. Our action will result in a direct confrontation with the Imperialist Navy of the United States. We will avenge the sinking of our destroyer in 2025 and the sabotage that destroyed the Gorae in 2026!"

Shouts of "Death to the Imperialists" resonated off the sixty-foot ceiling of the hall.

Hong Song-goi Tukmu-Sanga, the fleet's chief petty officer, had been Song-gil's loyal assistant for over twenty years and had picked every member of the assembled crew.

He addressed all of them. "Park Song-gil's own man, Chungsa Seung-Hyun-ju, is aboard the 092. After he opens the hatch, we will eliminate the personnel designated by Lieutenant Commander Sojwa and Hyong Yong-chol as unpatriotic and dangerous to our mission. That will include all the Chinese Navy personnel trainers."

Kim Yo Jong's bellicose rhetoric had belied her fears about any pitched battle where the KPN would lose even more vessels. Song-gil knew a cyberattack was planned for October 28, 2029. It involved a CIA-backed landing on Yeonpyeongdo in the Northern Limit disputed zone designed to disable the DPRK's—Democratic People's Republic of Korea's—MRBM—Medium Range Ballistic Missile—sites. His information indicated that South Korean forces would then reclaim the disputed territory. The man in charge of the KPN—Korean People's Navy—wanted to put their best asset in a position to threaten the United States, but his pleas to Kim Yo Jong for action turned her against him, so he had to act unilaterally.

Song-gil's contingent of twenty heavily armed conspirators moved quickly toward where the *Changzheng* 092 was docked. The sub was scheduled for a deep-sea patrol the next day—a milk run. Still, it was fully stocked, staffed, and armed. The men aboard who were loyal to Song-gil would do as he instructed. Since the training period had ended, they were more than capable of operating the vessel.

No one suspected any internal move. Consequently, there were only two sentries, and both had been sipping from a bottle of contraband Japanese whiskey. They were dead before they knew it—and without a sound. At the appointed time, 0220 hours, Chungsa Seung-Hyun-ju opened the hatch. Sojwa Hyon Yong-Chol went from compartment to compartment with Seung-Hyun-ju to eliminate all Haijun officers with the rank of Shao Xiao or higher whom he suspected might not cooperate with the scheme. He welcomed the new Daejang, Moon Song-gil, aboard, and they shoved off. Within minutes, they were below the surface and slipped out of the Mayang-do harbor, undetected and deadly.

25'

October 23, 2029, 1924 hours
USS ASW CG-71
Captain Denton Tracks the 092
Cape St. George, Western Pacific Ocean

Aboard his flagship, the USS *Cape St. George,* Captain Russ Denton scanned the intelligence report from the seventh Fleet Command in Yokosuka, Japan, and set his coffee mug down with a thump.

"Something wrong, Skip?" XO Roger Quinn asked.

"Not much," Denton answered. "We've just apparently let the only decent submarine in the entire North Korean Navy slip out of port in the middle of the night."

"What the hell?"

"Still waiting on details, but early analysis of satellite images looks like a hijacking," Denton explained. "My money would be on that crazy bastard Song-gil."

"The one they tried to kill after the regime change?"

"The very same."

Quinn whistled. "Does he know anything about skippering a nuclear boat?"

"From what I've read about him, the guy could sail everything from the *Pequod* to an aircraft carrier."

"Well, we all know what happened to Captain Ahab." Quinn laughed.

"Good point," Denton said. "But the son of a bitch caused a lot of mayhem before he went down with the ship."

§§

It didn't take long to find the missing sub. The JMSDF—Japanese Maritime Self Defense Force—hydrophone arrays were sensitive, accurate, and backed up by the US Fish-Hook Undersea Defense Line. The US-Japan network of underwater surveillance systems had been specifically designed to monitor Chinese and North Korean submarines in the East and South China Seas. The *Aki*, the newest Hibiki-class ship deploying the Surveillance Towed Array Sensor System—SURTASS—had located a C-3 within a hundred miles of its departure from Mayang-do.

"Got to be the one we're looking for," Denton pointed out. "At watch change last night, we knew where all the Chinese boats were."

"Damn good thing we found her so quick, Skip," Quinn remarked.

"Ya think?" Denton asked. "I mean, geez, it was the only boat we're supposed to be watching. I feel pretty stupid."

"Hey, don't beat yourself up. The CIA said she wasn't due to sail until five hours from now. How could you know someone would take her out early?"

Denton grinned without humor. "Nice sucking up, Quinn." His face relaxed. "Seriously, I appreciate the support. Now let's go chase her down."

Denton had shadowed the 092 on three other occasions—every time at sea. He never got close enough to pose a threat, and the enemy vessel never made any evasive maneuvers. He had no intention to be so coy this time. Something was wrong, and he needed to figure it out.

He looked across the bridge. "All ahead full. Pedal to the metal." He nodded to the Communications Officer. "Tell Sparky to let the *Milus,* the *Mason,* and the *Pegasus* know what's what."

Up top, the two guided-missile destroyers made the necessary adjustments. Two hundred miles away, the P-8A Poseidon *Pegasus,* a multi-mission maritime patrol and reconnaissance aircraft carrying anti-submarine ordnance, finished refueling and banked toward the ships.

Sparky sang out. "Skip, the only North Korean or Chinese boat unaccounted for is deep in the Sea of Japan bearing 043°—got to be the 092."

And the chase got serious.

26

October 23, 2029, 2100 Hours
Cape St. George, Western Pacific Ocean

Although new to North Korea, the 092 had only come into their possession because the Chinese Navy deemed it "too old to be useful." The sub had been commissioned in 1983 and then undergone a six-year remediation program before it was cleared for littoral service in 2009. It might have been decrepit by China's standards, but the North Koreans loved what to them was a shiny new toy, one capable of launching shiny new missiles loaded with nuclear warheads.

The BPIs aboard all three American ships promised boost phase intercepts at distances of over 750 kilometers. Almost instantaneous launch notifications and targeting were provided by the slew of new LEO and MEO satellites. They utilized precision tracking space sensors—PTSS—that provided functional targeting solutions within twenty seconds of launch. If the boost phase was the standard 180 seconds of solid-fueled ICBMs, the kill rate was still substantial if the interceptor was launched in a timely manner from a nearby location. If the boost phase was as long as the 250 seconds required for liquid-based ICBMs, the booster kill range nearly doubled.

Despite the experimental SM-3 Block IIBs' effectiveness in BPIs, due to the characteristics of the booster, liquid fuel, and twenty-seven-inch diameter, which required a unique launcher, the DOD only accepted 250 missiles before cancellation. Despite the Navy's ban on liquid-fueled missiles aboard Navy ships, by order of the President and the Secretary of Defense, the *Milius* was carrying twelve SM-3 Block IIBs to effect BPI intercepts on the 092.

If the intercept failed during the boost and post-boost-ascent phases, the integrated seamless tracking sensors operated by the C2BMC personnel in Colorado Springs throughout the flight transferred control to various mid-course interceptors and terminal phase interceptors.

It seemed to the Chinese and Russians that the entire purpose of the "The Golden Dome for America "system was to eliminate any second-strike capability. Given the potential effectiveness of more than eighty-six Ground-Based Midcourse Defense—GMD—missiles of the Ballistic Missile Defense System—BMDS—the Aegis mid-course SM-3 Block IIA system, the Aegis ashore system, and the addition of numerous other ABM terminal phase systems like the Iron Dome, they had legitimate worries.

Due to mutual mistrust, the US ABM systems served as a catalyst for a new arms race. In the minds of the communists, those systems had obliterated the doctrine of mutually assured destruction, considering what (if anything) would be left after a massive, overwhelming US first strike of a minimal deterrence force. While the United States maintained that ABM systems were to protect against rogue nations such as Iran and North Korea and not against second strikes by China and Russia, the system's effectiveness was originally somewhere between those two extremes. But by 2029, the US ABM system was considered robust and extremely effective by any standard. It had received a significant boost from AI modeling developed under Stargate.

The mainstay of the Aegis system, the SM-3 Block IIA missiles, had a range of 2,100 km, a speed of 5.5 km/s, and a maximum altitude of two thousand km. But when the Missile Defense Agency—MDA—announced the addition of numerous Terminal High Altitude Area Defense—THAAD—missile sites and numerous Arrow-5 and PAC sites to the Ballistic Missile Defense System, the defensive phase of the arms race was underway. The THAAD system could fire seventy-two interceptors from each squadron with a two hundred km range and a speed of ten km/s. The projectiles could reach an altitude of 150 km to destroy their targets and had demonstrated a 100 percent success rate in controlled tests. The ABM system's effectiveness against Chinese hypersonic glide vehicles was highly dependent on terminal phase intercepts.

China had been skittish, but its skittishness now gave way to paranoia.

27

October 23, 2029
The ABM Race and the 092 Threat

The fear seizing every nuclear nation by the throat had set off another arms race in the early 2000s after the United States withdrew from the Anti-Ballistic Missile Treaty. Over the next two decades, the Russians attempted to match American developments with numerous mid-course and terminal-phase intercept systems.

In November 2021, the Russians announced their new S-550 system, designed for satellite and ICBM intercepts as an addition to their already robust S-500 system that utilized surface-to-air missiles. They could detect and engage up to ten ballistic targets at speeds up to seven km/s at a distance of six hundred km and an altitude of two hundred km. The new 550 system increased engagement distance and altitude to twelve hundred and eight hundred km, respectively.

The Soviet A-235 PL-19 Nudol system presented a layered capability using the 51T missile and the Don 2NP/5N20P radar. It would intercept incoming ICBMs up to fifteen hundred km away at altitudes exceeding eight hundred km. The A-235 utilized the 53T6 missile for longer distances or the 45T6 missile for shorter range encounters. On February 4, 2026, when the United States failed to renew the New Start Treaty, panic crept across China.

Even with all these defenses, the *Changzheng* 092 transfer to North Korea presented a serious provocation, one that the Russians were compelled to answer. The transfer energized the defensive arms race between the Russians and the United States at a time when the Chinese, despite all their economic gains, could not compete with the

United States and Russia in the technological area of ABM warfare. Putin had learned about the submarine transfer too late to stop it. Privately, he chastised Xi Jinping for making a move destined to accelerate the US ABM program and encourage such a drastic increase in US ABM systems to threaten Russian and Chinese second-strike capabilities. Putin blamed Xi for the Golden Dome system that had proven to be very effective in intercepting ICBBs in the ascent and mid-course phase. So effective in fact that it had US military leaders talking about taking out North Korea effectively daring the Chinese to do anything about it.

President Armstrong's predecessor, Donald Trump, was outraged by the transfer of the 092 and took to the national airwaves time and time again to warn the Chinese. "Any missile launched from the *Changzheng,* regardless of the crew, will be treated as if it has originated in China."

The other two North Korean SSBs were old, remodeled Romeo-class submarines with three Pukguksong-3 missiles dropped in through an enlarged sail. Those six missiles were not deemed a material threat to the United States because of their short range, relatively light payload, and lack of a reliable reentry system.

But the remodeled Xia-class 092 SSBN reportedly carried 12 JL-1A missiles with a range of twenty-five hundred km that could be sequentially launched from a submerged platform in less than two minutes. The JL-1A RV had a 250—500 kt warhead, more than twenty times more powerful than the atomic bombs dropped on Hiroshima and Nagasaki. Armstrong instructed the ODNI that he wanted to know about any movements of the 092 in his DPB.

28

Saturday, October 27, 2029
Daily Presidential Briefing (DPB)
Oval Office, The White House
Washington, DC

President Connor Armstrong was on the eighth tee when the Daily Presidential Briefing landed on his desk in the Oval Office. Unlike his predecessors, Armstrong wanted a paper copy, believing that electronic interception was still possible despite the many safeguards in place. Armstrong typically scanned rather than read the DPM. By late afternoon, he got to it and noticed on the third page that the Special Collection Service—SCS—had intercepted numerous distress calls from the KPN to what had been designated the C-3 by Naval Intelligence. Armstrong called the Chief of Naval Operations, Admiral Gilday.

"What is a C-3, and why would there be a distress call to a C-3?" the President asked.

Gilday rolled his eyes. *Wish the hell this guy would provide some context, but that would require thinking on his part.* "Mr. President, it's an unidentified submarine."

Armstrong paused and thought out loud. "Why would the KPN—" he stopped. "By the way, what is the KPN?"

Gilday considered retirement for a second. "Mr. President, that is the Korean People's Navy, as in North Korea, and I have no idea why they would be issuing a distress call to an unidentified sub. But the junk they call a submarine is probably unable to surface, and they are attempting a rescue. That is as good of a guess as I can make without more intel."

Gilday would soon find out how wrong he was.

29

October 28, 2029
Denton Continues Pursuit
North Pacific Ocean

Captain Russ Denton had been shadowing the 092 for four days. The sub had stopped dead in the water a few times, only to proceed flat out at twenty-two knots again. Strange behavior.

On day five, Denton received a report from Lieutenant Bradley, who was flying the *Pegasus*.

"Captain, we have a contact on the submarine designated C-3 in your comms," Bradley reported. "Our APY-10 radar confirms the suspicions in your previous reports. It's the 092 Xia-class, hull number 406. It's on a heading of 087° at a speed of twenty-two knots, submerged at a depth of a hundred meters. If we're right, it will be within missile range of all cities located on the West Coast of the United States in two hours or less."

Denton wasted no time. "Deploy the sonobuoys around it for targeting."

An hour later, the sonobuoys were in the water, and the 092 had stopped within the sonobuoy perimeter.

The Chinese had added several enhancements to the 092 before giving it away. One was the ability to fire its submerged missiles in a shorter period. For reference, Denton kept in mind that the Ohio-class US SSBN could fire twenty MIRVED missiles in under six minutes. The *Changzheng* continued to test Denton's patience by darting in and out of the sonobuoy perimeter.

Captain Denton knew the drill. The 092 was a flashpoint in international relations. Dealing with its shenanigans required more authority than he possessed.

"Contact the Vice Admiral and ask for instructions," Denton ordered.

The scene had been played out many times in the Pacific over the past six months. But ever since Chairman Kim Jong Un's deadly illness in 2027 and Kim Yo Jong's bloody coup when she eliminated her older sister Kim Jong Chul, her nieces and nephews, and their mother, Ri Sol-ju, North Korea had become even more hegemonic.

Vice Admiral Fred Kuntz's chief of staff responded. "Continue to monitor closely. Keep your eighty-kilometer distance and take no provocative actions."

Typical. Sit on my hands and hope nothing kicks me in the balls.

The United States had prepared for threats from ballistic missiles by installing low Earth orbiting—LEO—and medium Earth orbiting—MEO—satellites, which created a detection network for ballistic missile launches. The system passed tracking and targeting information to the SM-3 Block IIA and SM-3 Block IIB missiles through Aegis Spy 6 (V) (4) onboard sensors.

In the event of a launch, the information was immediately given to the C2BMC in Colorado Springs. The C2BMC system also integrated the AN/TPY-2 and Spy-7(V1) sensor systems into its detection and fire control solutions for all phases, including the terminal defense batteries comprised of THAAD, THAAD-ER, AEGIS, ASHORE, SM-6 Block IB missiles, Arrow-5 missiles, Typhoon batteries, and PAAC-4/PAAC-5 systems.

And everything was about to be tested to the max.

30

October 28, 2029
North Pacific Ocean

The terror in the sonar operator's voice made Denton flinch.

"Skip, she broke hard east—like a sprinter coming out of the blocks. She's down to max depth of 270 meters and three kilometers past the sonobuoy perimeter."

What the hell!

Captain Denton shouted orders to Quinn. "Contact command in Yokosuka for permission to engage."

Denton turned to his intelligence officer, Lieutenant Junior Grade Matt Drollinger. "Send this report up the chain quickly. I don't want my ass on the line if this goes south."

The 092 continued east while Central Command twiddled their fingers.

§§

October 28, 2029
Yokosuka Naval Base
7th Fleet Command Center

Vice Admiral Fred Kuntz wasn't about to give engagement orders three months short of retirement. *I'm not starting World War III during my last deployment.* He turned when his chief of staff, Commander Wooten Croft, interrupted his thoughts.

"Admiral, the 092 has broken decisively east and is more than three kilometers outside the sonobuoys. Do you think we should include Admiral Stricter?"

Kuntz bristled. "No, Commander, and I'm not sinking it in international waters to give the Chinese an excuse to fire on our ships in the Taiwan Strait. Send the message."

31

October 28, 2029
Saanvi Wali Monitors 092 Reports
ODNI 1500 Tysons McLean Drive
McLean, Virginia

Saanvi Wali had been monitoring the situation in the North Pacific with her staff for the last twenty-four hours. She called Admiral Gilday at the Pentagon.

"Admiral, we've got a problem. If the 092 gets within range, NSA is convinced it will fire on our West Coast. The signals from Pyongyang indicate they have lost control of the boat."

"Based on what?" Gilday asked.

"Based on the feud between Kim Yo Jong and Fleet Admiral Moon Song-gil," Saanvi stated. "Admiral Song-gil is missing. North Korea's National Intelligence Service thinks Kim Yo Jong ordered his execution, and the Admiral reacted by hijacking the 092."

Gilday buried his face in his hands. *Oh my God, she is the ops chief at ODNI. Armstong and the whole bunch will start a nuclear war.*

After taking a moment to collect himself, Gilday replied. "Well, Wali, maybe Kim Yo Jung can shoot better than you think she can. If the Admiral is dead—"

Saanvi's voice barked through the headset.

"Admiral, we need to contain this situation *now*."

Saanvi knew Gilday had virtually ignored every report she'd filed on the 092 for the past six months.

"Admiral, the ODNI believes the Chinese PLAN was in control of the boat until the twenty-third of this month. Have you read the Admiral's profile?"

"In my estimation, he may be a radical, but he's a minor threat," Gilday growled.

"Sure," Saanvi snapped. "And twenty years ago, you probably thought Taylor Swift was just another teeny-bopper flash in the pan."

"Ms. Wali, we have other issues of much more importance—"

Saanvi exploded. "I know you think I'm some hysterical woman, but I'm not screwing around here. We have satellite pictures of twenty individuals boarding the sub and casting off. We can clearly see two dead sentries. I'll say this very slowly, so you'll understand. An authorized individual would not need to murder a couple of guards."

Gilday began to sputter. "There's no reason to be insulting, Ms. Wali."

"No, sir," she said. "Nor is there an excuse for acting like a little kid, covering your eyes and claiming you're invisible. This is not a drill, and it sure as hell isn't a children's game. Admiral Song-gil is the only North Korean naval officer with enough balls to steal a nuclear sub from his own country. He's a true believer. His own government is hunting him. That means he's pissed and has nothing to lose. Once he gets that boat close enough, he *will* fire on the United States because he wants to take out as many people as he can and because the act will guarantee the destruction of the countrymen who are trying to kill him. You can keep screwing around, but I'm headed to the White House."

32

October 28, 2029
North Korean 092 Fires Twelve Missiles

The North Koreans often blamed US sabotage for their own ineptness. On May 23, 2025 the North Koreans tried to launch an advanced missile destroyer from their naval base in Chongjin only to have it break in half. The North Koreans had only produced one Sinpo-class submarine—SSB—the Gorae. For undetermined reasons, it exploded in 2026 while on patrol and contaminated a 1,550-square-mile section of the Pacific. The North Koreans blamed the U.S. Navy and threatened nuclear retaliation against South Korea with the means to accomplish it.

For the next three years, the U.S. Navy has walked on eggshells, reluctant to provoke the erratic KPN. The North Koreans continued to test-fire submarine-based and land-based missiles but were careful to ensure nothing landed anywhere near the United States. But they regularly terrorized their neighbors by firing missiles over Japanese airspace. The acquisition of the 092 constituted a clear and present danger in its present position.

Denton decided to take more aggressive steps and ordered a second set of sonobuoys. They were deployed with P-8A drop warning depth charges. The sub came to a full stop and rose to a depth of a hundred meters. Denton heaved a sigh of relief but remained apprehensive about the sub's intentions in light of the recent escalating rhetoric between Kim Yo Jong and President Armstrong. Then the 092 moved again. Bradley was following all this on his comm and expected the worst. *It's going to come up to thirty meters and fire. Just stopped on its way up.*

Sure enough, the 092 came up to a depth of less than thirty meters and stopped again, the optimal depth for firing the JL-1A. It stayed there too long to satisfy Denton. Denton moved to the bridge. "Put Bradley on my comm on the bridge."

A distress call came in from Lieutenant Bradley on the P-8A. "First missile out of tube-clearing water. Other missiles follow at fifteen-second intervals."

Denton's life had come down to this moment, and he flinched. "Give me the direction of the first missile, Lieutenant Bradley."

"Still straight up, now bending southeast. More missiles are clearing water. Repeat several missiles away. Spray pattern ranging from 52 to 110 degrees. Appear to be bending east. More missiles coming out of tubes."

What is he waiting for? Bradley thought.

Denton did not hesitate this time. Absent orders from Yokosuka and risking court martial, he barked out lethal instructions to his crew. "Engage SM-3 Block IIB anti-ballistic missiles. We need to get those bastards in the next three minutes. Have the *Milius* fire SM-IIB BPI interceptors now!" He radioed Bradley, "Take out that damn sub!"

"Roger that," Bradley responded. Seconds later, the *Pegasus* launched two MK-54 torpedoes.

"Torpedoes in the water running true and direct," Bradley stated. "ECM from 092 ineffective. Mk-54 speed is thirty-eight knots. Expect impact in thirty-seven seconds."

The last missile from the 092 had just cleared the surface when the MK-54 torpedo disintegrated its bow section.

Bradley could not keep the excitement out of his voice. "Target destroyed!"

The cheering stopped abruptly with his next statement, this one somber and strained.

"Those missiles are headed straight for the US West Coast." Bradley groaned.

33

October 28, 2029
Schriever Space Force Base
Colorado Springs, Colorado

The first missile had cleared the water and been in the air for only ten seconds before alarms went off at Schriever Space Force Base in Colorado Springs. Fifteen seconds later, Lieutenant General Jon Carpenter knew this wasn't a drill. He had the men he wanted in the room.

Carpenter had attended numerous high-level meetings where he had fought hard for Colonel Vernon Axelrod and Major Emmitt Spires to be the Agency's decision-makers in the event of an attack on the United States. The men had refused promotions up the chain of command to remain in their positions. They devoted every waking hour to coordinating how to handle a situation where millions of lives were at stake.

Axelrod had a background in electrical engineering from Purdue University and had received PhDs from Stanford in both mathematics and physics. Spires was a programmer. He had developed code for linking all the MDA's computers responsible for handling detection, tracking, and targeting utilizing quantum computing concepts. Spires had developed quantum circuits that sorted the qubits into specific quantum gates. Then he integrated the entire system with his unique coding skills, enabling the MDA system to make corrections for missiles while numerous missiles from the same Aegis ship were in flight.

Carpenter heard the alarm and ran to the command post. "Gentlemen, we've got nukes in the air from a commie sub. Figure out what we should do—PDQ!"

An eerie calm settled over the elevated circular platform ringing the C2BMC center. Everyone could clearly discern the preliminary alarm, with audible and visual signals indicating the 092 launch of twelve Jl-1As ten seconds after they cleared the water. Axelrod began reading the instructions aloud. For anyone not in the know, he might as well have been going over the steps for assembling an Ikea nightstand.

"Bring LEO-23 to an inclination of sixty degrees and adjust the eccentricity to give us a better picture of the direction of those missiles. Prepare to transfer targeting and firing sequence on my command."

"Any chance this is a mistake?" Spires asked.

"This is hostile action," Axelrod said emphatically.

34

October 28, 2029
Situation Room, The White House
Washington, DC

President Armstrong had just gotten to his chair at the head of the table in the Situation Room when Saanvi Wali spoke. She had come straight to the Sit Room from the Pentagon. "A few minutes ago, ICBMs were launched from a nuclear submarine. The targets appear to be Portland, San Francisco, and Los Angeles. The missiles' statuses remain undetermined, but it appears we have about fifteen minutes to act."

There was so little color in the President's face that he appeared transparent. His youthful bravado was gone. He was suddenly aware that he was the President of the United States and was expected to do something. Following a brief discussion, it was the consensus to take the staff to the bunker—the Presidential Emergency Operations Center.

On his way out of the Situation Room, Rockton stopped and whispered to Saanvi. "We're in a world of shit. See if you can do anything. He's so out of his depth, he can't see the bottom of the pool."

Armstrong was muttering to himself. When he looked up, Saanvi was right next to him.

"Suggestions?" he asked, looking at her.

"Mr. President, first things first. We have to knock down the missiles."

"Of course, of course," Armstrong nodded. "Makes perfect sense."

"Axelrod is already on that, sir," Saanvi said.

"What about after?" Armstrong asked.

"We assess the damage," Saanvi ordered. "Regardless, at the moment, all twelve warheads are targeted and might be intercepted."

Armstrong scowled. "What's the latest status on the warheads?"

"We'll see when we get to the PEOC. But my bet is that the stragglers have been hit by the *Milius* in the ballistic phase."

35

October 28, 2029
PEOC Bunker, The White House
Washington, DC

Many gathered in the bunker.

Saanvi Wali.

Samantha Trimer.

John Rockton.

Admiral Christopher Grady, Chairman of the JCS.

Admiral Michael Gilday, CNO.

General Matt Brown, Chief of Staff, USAF.

General Lori Griffin, Deputy Secretary of Defense.

General Glen VanHerck, Commander of North American Aerospace Defense Command—NORAD.

General James McConville, Chief of Staff, U.S. Army.

Michael J. Lewis, Assistant Director DOD, specialist on China's nuclear arsenal.

Benton Hostetler, advisor to the President.

President Connor Armstrong and his family.

The electric locks on the bunker slid into place and clanged shut. While First Lady Emily Armstrong tended to the children, everyone else stared at a blank screen and waited for a report from Admiral

Grady, who assumed the role of narrator. His voice was strained as he pointed to tracking displays on the monitors.

"*Milius* has engaged an automatic firing solution for SM-3IIBs. They were activated within the requisite sixty seconds. We have prepared mid-course intercepts for all Aegis-capable ships in range and SM-6B Block I Sea-Based Terminal Defense ships for the three DDGs lining the West Coast."

Six blips on the screens suddenly disappeared.

"What happened?" Armstrong asked.

"The *Milus* knocked out six SLBMs from the 092 in the ballistic phase."

Armstrong pumped his fist. "Yes!"

The Admiral shook his head. "I wouldn't get too excited, Mr. President. That was easy. We've still got six incoming enemy projectiles. Here's where it gets very tricky."

Armstrong tried to sound presidential. "Admiral, what are we doing about the remaining missiles?"

Colonel Vernon Axelrod, the expert in Colorado Springs, answered from screen one. "The remaining RVs are exothermic. Speed 3.8 kilometers per second, altitude 250 kilometers. The apogee will be 750 kilometers. The targets are Los Angeles, San Francisco, and Portland. Nine SM-3 Block IIA interceptors are acquiring targets and have just been launched from three destroyers."

The President watched the intercept missiles approach their targets on screens three through eight. Three more JL-1As were destroyed by Aegis SM-3 Block IIA missiles at various altitudes of five hundred to seven hundred km by the kinetic EKVs from the *Pinckney* DDG-91, the *Momsen* DDG-92, and the *Stockdale* DDG-106.

"That is it for the Aegis assets we have in place. The other three will have to be knocked down with our terminal defense system. The remaining three keep hurtling through the sky, one toward each of the three targeted cities." Axelrod gave an update.

"How good is that?" the President asked Axelrod.

"Very good, Mr. President, but in this business, nothing is certain. I will tell you more in a moment. Right now, I'm busy with the terminal intercept system."

Armstrong dropped his face into his hands, like President Kennedy did when he was told about the Russian subs during the Ex-Com meetings sixty-seven years earlier. *Who the hell would want this job? Will I be compared to Lyndon Johnson, who famously declined a second term?*

Secretary of Defense John Rockton glanced across the table at Admiral Gilday, who knew the Aegis capabilities well. Rockton could tell by Gilday's worried look that they were in for a lengthy stay in the PEOC.

Armstrong's voice was a mere whisper. "Secretary. Are all forces at DEFCON 2?"

Rockton didn't even look up. "All forces to DEFCON 2."

The nuclear football was on the President's left. *At least he didn't leave it in the Situation Room*, Saanvi thought. All US airborne bombers were deadheaded for their POC—point of control—locations. NATO had been alerted, and China and the Soviet Union were bracing for the worst while hoping that the terminal US ABM system was even better than they had imagined.

"Mr. President…" Major Spires chimed in on screen one. "All three cities have THAAD-ER-PAC-5, Arrow, and Typhoon batteries. They have transitioned their AN/TPY-2 launch to a remote OPIR radar, allowing us to control the targeting over to our system. I have engaged our internal automatic fire control system for all batteries.

Only the terminal systems in the targeted cities can help. None of the other THAAD, Typhoon, Arrow-5, and Aegis Ashore systems are within range of these trajectories."

When Saanvi heard Spires' voice, she felt a rush of adrenaline jolt her body. She looked up at the screen. *This can't be.*

"What now?" Armstrong asked. He winced when he heard his voice crack a little.

"We wait, sir," Rockton said. "It now depends on how good our terminal systems are in stopping the remaining three missiles."

36

October 28, 2029
PEOC, The White House
Washington, DC

They did not have to wait long. The THAAD-ER system intercepted the warheads headed for Los Angeles and San Francisco just outside the atmosphere at an altitude of 105 km, thirty miles from the coastline. The terminal phase systems in the Northwest outside Portland performed flawlessly but missed the remaining warhead. It had been grazed by an SM-Block IIA ABM and began to tumble like Hoyt Wilhelm's knuckle ball.

Axelrod swore. "Hitting that thing now is going to be like trying to knock a gnat out of the air with a chopstick."

Every gaze locked onto screen eight and watched the fluttering warhead wobble toward the last Patriot battery.

"Goddamn thing doesn't fly straight," the President criticized.

"Damn inconsiderate," Rockton mumbled under his breath. He despised the young, cocky, underinformed, shallow politician. He considered him a perfect reflection of the American people's growing tendency to bypass qualified but slightly dull candidates in favor of glittery men and women who spoke loudly and long before they bothered to engage their brains, if they had one.

The enemy missile disappeared from the screen.

"What happened?" Armstrong asked.

"Mr. President," Axelrod swallowed before continuing. "The knuckling of the warhead made it land east of Portland. We'll have casualties. Just not as many as we thought."

Armstrong looked perturbed and muttered to no one in particular 'and to think we spent a trillion on Trump's "Golden Dome for America" what a waste'

§§

Columbia River Gorge
35 Miles NNE of Portland, Oregon

Major Emmitt Spires jumped in to assist Axelrod since he was more familiar with the blast and radiation effects. "From what we can see, the seven hundred kiloton thermonuclear explosion had a Ground Zero just south of the Hood River, not too far from downtown Stevenson, Washington, a town of fifteen hundred near the Oregon state line. It was a surface burst with a fireball radius of nearly three-quarters of a mile and a blast damage radius of one and a quarter miles. The radiation radius for five hundred REM, or Radiation Equivalent Man, where most people will die, is about one and a half miles. The thermal radiation effects are wider and will kill everyone outside up to six miles from Ground Zero. If we're careful, we should be able to hold the number killed to less than ten thousand."

Armstrong was relieved at first and then enraged to the point that Rockton thought briefly again about the Twenty-Fifth Amendment.

§§

PEOC, The White House
Washington, DC

President Armstrong turned to his two intelligence chiefs. Wali and Hostetler had anticipated his question and had consulted with their staff during the flurry of activities.

"Mr. President," Wali began. "To answer your question, the intelligence community can report that no other threats, foreign or domestic, are present at this time. But Russia is in executive session, and we're listening to their conversations. They're not contemplating any action, but China is in flux with their leaders, unsure of what to do next. You read the report I sent three days ago, concluding the likelihood that North Korean radicals took the 092 by force and have disposed of the Chinese officers in charge."

Armstrong nodded and stated in an uncharacteristically lucid and intelligent policy response, "Jinping knows that anything coming from the 092 is his responsibility—period."

Hostetler felt compelled to weigh in. "We feel that Russia will side with us on what happens next based on their statements to Xi Jinping about the irresponsible decision to transfer to Kim Yo Jong any nuclear weapons capable of hitting the United States."

37

October 28, 2029
PEOC, The White House
Washington, DC

Secretary of State Michael Johnston tapped the President on the shoulder. "Putin" was all he said. He pointed at a screen.

"Put him through," Armstrong ordered.

Russian Premier Vladimir Putin had lost his stoic, impenetrable visage. His eyes were wide, either with horror or fear, and his voice was higher than his normal grumble.

"Mr. President," Putin began. "Russia had nothing to do with the nuclear weapon that just struck the United States. We have no forces on alert. What can we do to help?"

Putin was relieved when he saw that President Armstrong, though pale, seemed in control and rational. Putin had feared he would encounter the bombastic showman whose campaign had electrified the United States.

"Premier Putin," Armstrong stated confidently. "The United States is not rushing to any judgment, but we will remain on full alert until this matter is sorted out. You can help yourself and us by providing all your intelligence on this issue within the next sixty minutes. I expect your full cooperation. Anything less will be considered an act of aggression and will have a very negative impact on your country."

Putin bridled for a moment. "Is that a threat, sir?" He immediately regretted his reaction.

"No, Vladimir," Armstrong eyed the man on the screen. "It's an absolute promise."

Putin took a beat to rein in his notorious temper. "Mr. President, I don't need an hour. I was extremely displeased with Chairman Jinping's decision to sell the 092 to North Korea. I even communicated my displeasure to Vice Premier Han Zheng. My sources tell me what you already know—the missiles were launched from that Chinese submarine. I can also assure you the Russian people want peace with the United States. We will not attack the United States unless you attack Russia first. As we speak, our main intelligence Service known to you as the GRU is sending probable launch locations for all mobile Chinese DF-41AGs. We will assist the United States in controlling the Chinese arsenal, but—and I ask this humbly—you must pledge not to resort to a first use of nuclear weapons."

Armstrong looked at Rockton, who nodded. "Fine," Armstrong said. "You know, we will retaliate for the attack. You would do the same. We will not use our nuclear arsenal against China unless they launch against us. Given that promise, I expect you to stand down and back us in any conventional action we take. Some time ago, my predecessor told Chairman Jinping that any missile launched from the 092 would be considered launched by China. He cannot escape the consequences by fighting a proxy war or hiding behind you. Have I made our position clear?"

"As clear as Rogaska," Putin stated.

Rockton had already scribbled a note by the time Armstrong looked at him. *Russian crystal.*

Putin continued. "Russia does not want to become the enemy of the United States at any time, especially today. My scientists have informed me that a large-scale nuclear exchange will exacerbate our already poor atmospheric conditions. I will work with you and Chairman Jinping to defuse this most unfortunate situation. All Russian submarines will surface and await a favorable outcome."

38

October 28, 2029
PEOC, The White House
Washington, DC

Armstrong took twenty minutes to consult with his senior advisors, ranking members of Congress, and military leaders. He looked at Rockton, who turned to Saanvi Wali. The two had devised a plan that might still prevent a nuclear war.

"Liquidate the Chinese Navy's nine SSBNs and sink its two aircraft carriers," Armstrong ordered. "Level all three Chinese military bases in the Taiwan Strait."

"What about the Chinese military personnel?" asked Gilday. "We're on the last rung here before a nuclear war starts."

"I care less about them than the Chinese do about the men, women, and children of Portland." Armstrong leaned in closer to Gilday. "If you want to give civilians in Taipei and Seoul a get-the-hell-out-of-Dodge warning, that's up to you. But then I want you to obliterate everyone in North Korea who wears a uniform."

"Yes, sir."

Armstrong pointed at his defense secretary. "Those sons of bitches in North Korea get no warning. Got it?"

"Roger that, sir."

President Armstrong ordered more personnel to the bunker under the East Wing.

§§

While Mrs. Armstrong played games with the children, everyone else stared at a blank screen and waited for a report from Admiral Stricter, Commander of the U.S. Seventh Fleet. The Admiral's face appeared on the screen. On an adjacent screen was a spreadsheet.

"Mr. President," Admiral Stricter began. "Within the last hour and forty-five minutes, we have decimated the Chinese Navy. Take a look."

All heads turned to the report on the other screen.

- 096 Changzheng 22 422 SSBN sunk by Iowa MK-48 22'06"N, 180'17"E
- 096 Changzheng 24 424 SSBN sunk by Idaho MK-48 30'29"N, 165'22"E
- 094A Changzheng 21 421 SSBN sunk by Mass. MK-48 15'53"N, 116'07"E
- 094A Changzheng 20 421 SSBN sunk by Indiana MK-48 16'45"N, 115'21"E
- 094A Changzheng 14 414 SSBN sunk by J. Carter TmHK Yulin Naval Base
- 094A Changzheng 12 412 SSBN sunk by J. Carter TmHK Yulin Naval Base
- 094 Changzheng 13 413 SSBN sunk by J. Carter TmHK Yulin Naval Base
- 094 Changzheng 11 411 SSBN sunk by J. Carter TmHK Yulin Naval Base
- 001 Liaoning* 16 Aircraft Car sunk by DDG-85 NSM 25'34"N, 172'34"E
- 002 Shandong** 17 Aircraft Car sunk by DDG-54 NSM 17'22"N, 114'57"E

"Carriers *John F. Kennedy* and *Ronald Reagan* of the U.S. Seventh Fleet are securely tucked away behind a screen of destroyers and steaming for territory beyond the range of any Chinese ASCMs. The asterisks indicate hostile aircraft we shot down during the course of the engagement—thirty-seven in all. Several of the Chinese aircraft launched YU-12 ASMs. They did no damage. We have lost twelve aircraft. Rescue operations are underway. The three Chinese Island bases in the Taiwan Strait are smoking holes in the ground."

There was a murmur of satisfaction, but no one felt like cheering. The death toll tipped heavily on the other side.

The Admiral continued. "Seven Chinese destroyers launched YU-18 missiles. They are all now at the bottom of the ocean. They are as follows: *Nanchang* 101, *Lhasa* 102, *Dalian* 105, *Hefei* 174, *Xning* 117, *Hohhot* 161, and *Anshan* 103. China has fired over 100 DF-26B and DF-21E anti-ship ballistic missiles at our two carriers from their 634th, 676th, and 689th brigades in eastern China. Our ECM produced malfunctions in the reentry vehicles for nearly all warheads. The SM-6 Dual Block II intercept missiles destroyed any RVs that appeared as threats, not affected by our ECM. I would be remiss if I failed to mention the air superiority coverage by the F-47 NGAD from the Anderson Base on Guam. The fifty fighters stationed there took on a much larger force of JL-20Bs and engaged in numerous nonvisual engagements. They downed eight Jl-20Bs with AIM-120Ds before the remaining JL-20Bs bugged out."

Admiral Gilday was trying not to smile. "Thank you, Admiral Stricter. Remain vigilant and expect the worst."

Everyone turned to President Armstrong.

§§

The President remained silent for a while. He was scrutinizing preliminary reports from the Portland area. With each line of text, his face reddened. Without asking, the White House physician began monitoring the Chief Executive's blood pressure. Armstrong did not protest.

"The death toll is lighter than we expected." Armstrong paused. "But one American death is too many. Now we have eight thousand." He looked up. "What can we expect from Chairman Jinping, and what are their land-based missile capabilities?"

Michael J. Lewis, a Chinese weapons expert from the Pentagon and an Assistant Secretary of Defense, presented his report. Everyone listened, but on the other side of the world, a more interesting conversation was taking place in Beijing, where Jinping and his top six committee members were in conference with Putin and his defense ministers.

39

October 29, 2029
Beijing, China

The Central Military Commission of China recommended a declaration of war on the United States to the Politburo Standing Committee of the Chinese Communist Party. Jinping and Vice Chairman Han Zheng wanted to enlist the support of the Russian Federation. Putin was expecting the call and wanted information on the aftermath.

Putin and Defense Minister Andrey Belousov met with Nikolai Dolgushkin and Alexander Sergeev, two atmospheric scientists from the Russian Academy of Sciences, to discuss the latest findings from computer models on the potential consequences of a nuclear war between the United States and China. They had already told Putin such a war would have an extremely detrimental effect on Russian agriculture.

"The nuclear winter theory is no longer accurate," Sergeev reported. He wasn't sure he was right, but he'd been told what to say. "Such a war will most likely deplete seventy to eighty percent of the ozone filter in the atmosphere and result in worldwide disease and famine. For each megaton exploded at the optimal HOB, we can expect five thousand tons of nitric oxides to be carried into the upper atmosphere. The soot promotes the formation of nitrogen oxides and nitrogen dioxide, which combine with O3 molecules. The resulting chemical reaction will deplete the O3 molecules that form the protective ozone layer."

Murmurs filled the room. Putin waved them quiet and faced the screen. "Spare me the science. How long will this last?"

"Between ten and fifteen years." Dolgushkin didn't blink.

§§

Putin greeted the seven-member Chinese Politburo like long-lost relatives. "Good evening, my friends. We're up-to-date on the actions in the Pacific. We urge you to respond with restraint and join us in a call for a ceasefire before more blood is shed."

Chairman Jinping's face twisted in rage. "How can we do that after the Americans have slaughtered fifteen thousand of our brave servicemembers and destroyed our Navy? We must have a proportionate response. We must sink the *John F. Kennedy* and the *Ronald Reagan*."

"Any attempt on the carriers will cause the United States to hit you with more than two thousand megatons of nuclear weapons." Putin pointed his finger at Jinping. "China will cease to exist."

"They will not attack us," Jinping argued.

"My top advisors disagree," Putin shot back. Putin almost sneered. *I managed to manipulate an American President for eight years without so much as a derringer being fired. This dolt is about to blow us to bits.*

"Then we will retaliate on our own." Chairman Jinping was angry—or perhaps frightened. It was hard to tell.

Putin shook his head. "I cannot let you do that."

"What exactly are you saying?"

"We will knock your missiles down."

Jinping shrieked with disbelief. "You will fight against us?"

Putin's legendary temper boiled over. He screamed at the images on the screen. "You idiots were instructed not to sell the 092 to North

Korea. You're getting off lightly compared to what is going to happen in North Korea. If you persist, the atmosphere will be contaminated for years, which will have an extremely detrimental effect on Russia's food supply. We can't let that happen. We're informing the United States that we will employ all our ABM forces, including the S-550, to knock down your missiles after launch." He paused for dramatic effect and then punctuated each word with a jabbing finger. "*Do. Not. Fire. Any. Ballistic. Missiles. At. America.*"

Even though the North Koreans had fought alongside Russia in Ukraine, Putin was willing to turn his back on North Korea under the circumstances. He had already refused to take any calls from Kim Yo Jong.

Jinping continued to rant. "What if the United States attacks us?"

Putin calmed a bit. "We will defend you if the United States uses nuclear weapons against you first. But if you commence the hostilities, we're not your friend."

Xi snorted. "You never were a true communist."

Whatever remaining self-control Putin had suddenly dissolved. "I'm telling you to stand down! You underestimate the destruction NATO missiles will bring. In addition, India will strike you with hundreds of their new sub- and land-based nuclear missiles. We will not join you in a first strike. You will struggle to get any of your missiles through the combined ABM systems of the United States and Russia. Any missiles entering Russian airspace will be knocked down and treated as a hostile act. We know the general location of your rail- and truck-mounted mobile launchers. The S-550 will take out most of your liquid-fueled DF-5C MIRVs in the ascent phase. Do not press us on this issue, or you will die within fifteen minutes of your launch."

The sun on the Russia-China relationship had been inexorably setting ever since Jinping refused to support Russia with troops in its failed attempt to annex Ukraine in 2022. Putin blamed Jinping for not sending weapons and soldiers when Russia was in dire need. Putin was sure a nuclear war with the United States and NATO would be the end of the world. He hoped Jinping would soon come to his senses and think of another way to punish the United States. He advised Jinping to sell all his country's bonds and cripple the US economy, a move certain to cause tremendous economic turmoil.

Putin's jaw twitched. He snarled at the screen. "Because of your stupidity, thousands will die. You have already killed Americans in the Northwestern United States. Unlike you, the United States does not consider its people expendable pawns. You should suffer the consequences of your actions, and you need to reflect on the large disparity in nuclear warheads and the AI-ABM defense advancements. If you fire first, the FSB has determined that the United States is likely to stop all your warheads. You're committing suicide!"

Enraged, Jinping terminated the feed and turned to the members of the Standing Committee and his military advisors. His voice screeched like an air raid siren.

"They're bluffing!"

No one spoke until General Wei Fenghe dared to say, "Mr. Chairman, I respectfully disagree. The Russians are doing what is in their own self-interest."

Before Jinping could respond, Chinese Air Force General Xu Qiliang and General Zhang Youxia joined in dissent. "We cannot launch our missiles against the United States. They have a ten-to-one advantage and a better ABM system. Even though it was not under our command, our submarine fired the first shot. World opinion and every other nuclear power on the planet will take action against us if we don't stop. We must contact the Americans and request a ceasefire. We may not be able to penetrate the Golden Dome that shields America "

Vice Premier Han Zheng jumped to his feet. "Enough from you military cowards! The Russians are bluffing. We must respond to imperialist aggression. If we don't, we will be seen as weaklings and be pushed around forever. I demand a vote from the Standing Committee. If we die, we will die with honor."

Li Zhanshu waited for the clamor to subside. "Comrades, if we go down the road suggested by Han Zheng, we will have violated our pledge of no first use. We will violate the alliance of the no-first-use countries' treaty we entered into last year. The other countries in the alliance—India, France, and Russia—will be obligated to defend the United States. We cannot travel such a perilous path. Our fight is with Moon Song-gil and the North Koreans who killed Yichen Zhang, our Hajun da Xi do, and his crew on the 092. But they are dead, and there is nothing we can do to them. Therefore, let us consider the business at hand."

He sat, and the voting commenced.

40

October 29, 2029
Moscow, Russia

After the feed was terminated in Moscow, some of the defense ministers became critical of Putin. Shoigu addressed them as if they were school children who had flunked first grade.

"The British Vanguard and S616 French Le Triomphant classes of SSBNs possess more than six hundred warheads," Shoigu chided. "Add those to the four thousand plus the Americans have added to their stockpile after dropping out of New Start. Each of those can be delivered to our homeland. At least five hundred will hit their targets. The Chinese, if they ignore the danger, will launch nearly half of their stockpile of 450 nuclear warheads against the United States. The British and especially the French will stand clear but remain on alert. If we launch with the Chinese, all of NATO will fire on us within ninety seconds. Whose missiles would you prefer to defend against?"

Putin nodded, dismissing the Jominian prattle from the hawkish generals. Military leaders around the globe, except China, showed little appreciation for what a post-nuclear-war world would look like.

§§

October 28, 2029
PEOC, The White House
Washington, DC

While Putin reamed Xi Jinping, Michael J. Lewis, Pentagon weapons expert, continued his briefing. "The Chinese will place the limited number of W-88 type warheads on their two best missiles, the DF-

41A and the DF-5C. They both have a range of seventeen thousand kilometers even when carrying three warheads. If they launch, the entire United States will be within range of most of their missiles, regardless of whether they utilize a polar or a west-east trajectory. They've upgraded over the last three years and can probably attack us without flying their missiles over Russia. But they may attempt to fly over Russian airspace, risking Russian intercepts. That is one situation I can't handicap. Those upgrades are most likely the result of their desire to have sufficient range to attack the United States without a Russian overflight."

All those in the room said nothing, and Lewis continued. "Russia's economic spiral almost toppled Putin. My contemporaries at the Agency estimate that the People's Liberation Army Rocket Force has approximately 425 to 500 warheads available on ICBMs, MRBMs, and IRBMs. Of the two hundred plus ICBMs located in range of the United States, about 150 are LOW capable."

"What's LOW?" It was a voice from the back. No one turned to embarrass the questioner.

"Launch on Warning," Lewis explained. "Read over the handout we're distributing. It outlines where the LOW ICBMS will be coming from—mostly silos in Yumen, Hami, and Hanggin. These missiles can boost three reentry vehicles into a predictable, ballistic missile path. They will employ chaff and decoys. Thanks to our AI upgrades, our ABM system has integrated an API interface that will eliminate the chaff from targeting. Our ABM system has shown an ability to learn on the fly. No pun intended. China's ABM system cannot match ours and will not intercept any of our Trident II missiles. We also believe the 644th Brigade in Hanzhong may have some newer DF-41AGs. These are highly mobile missiles that can be transported over rugged terrain."

Lewis gave everyone a chance to look over the handout. "The other major threat comes from the DF-5C. It's a bigger rocket and can carry ten MIRVed RVs. Most likely, they will come from Base 25 at Wuzhai, the 401st Brigade at Luoning, or Xuanhua. Even though it is liquid-fueled, it can be ready to go in as little as fifteen minutes. Several DF-5Cs are in the autonomous region of Tibet."

"What else?" Armstrong asked.

"Well…" Lewis paused. "The DF-31AG has been upgraded to a range of fifteen thousand kilometers. It's highly mobile, similar to the DF-41AG, and carries at least three warheads. Both the DF-41AG and the DF-31AG are solid-fueled. They need minimal prep time. The DF-31AG, like all Chinese missiles, is highly accurate, with a Circular Error Probability, or CEP, of 150 meters or less. The DF-41AG is considered the superior missile because the 31AG has more misfires, causing aborts."

"What about their IRBMs and MRBMs?" Armstrong asked.

Lewis was prepared. "Mr. President, Chinese IRBM and MRBM weapons can easily reach Guam, Japan, and South Korea. Taiwan alone has over two thousand missiles trained on it, and a handful of them carry nuclear warheads. Your red sheet identifies the types of missiles and other locations for People's Liberation Army Rocket Forces brigades in China known to have ICBMs."

President Armstrong took a breath. "Okay. What do we gain from a preemptive first strike?"

It felt like all the air had been sucked out of the subterranean room. Lewis was the only person who did not mentally flinch. "I wouldn't advise that."

Secretary of State Johnston was quick to blurt out in an excited tone, "I think we may have to then defend against Russia as well, and that is the end."

"Well, sir," Lewis glanced to Johnston. "I think you're right, but to answer the President's question, you may be able to knock out a third of their ICBMs and fifty percent of their shorter-range missiles at best before they launch. It all depends on where their missiles are when our warheads hit. At least that's my opinion."

"SAC should weigh in on this issue," Admiral Gilday added. "They're on screen now. General Dawkins believes we hold a huge advantage if we strike first against the Chinese. Our most effective first-strike weapon may be our B-21 fleet, but our closest base is more than two hours out. They could simultaneously eliminate many of the hard siloed targets without detection. In addition, the B-21s could take out the DF-5C liquid series of heavy payload rockets that are not fueled under these circumstances. We have no evidence that they have been or are being fueled. Even though they're silo-based, General Dawkins believes we can take them out before they can be fired."

41

October 28, 2029
PEOC, The White House
Washington, DC

There was a static crackle. Colonel Axelrod's face appeared on the center screen. "Mr. President, it's all moot now. Seconds ago, our LEO satellites detected over two hundred launches across China and 112 ICBMs at T-plus twelve. Expect more. We are taking control of the SM-3 Block IIB BPI missiles in Mongolia. We will be launch-ready in T-plus thirty seconds. All the northern-based Chinese ICBMs appear to be taking a circumpolar route and will enter Russian airspace. Those missiles will hit the United States from the north-northwest. Missiles launched from central and southern China will travel west to east and enter from the Pacific. All our ABM systems are up and ready, twenty-six to thirty-eight minutes to impact."

Axelrod took a breath and continued. "The missiles were fired from areas known to house ICBMs. Our Pacific Fleet of Aegis destroyers is well-positioned. Many of the missiles will come within the 2,100-kilometer range of the SM-3 Block IIAs onboard those ships. We have the three Zumwalt-class stealth destroyers in the Yellow Sea, the Sea of Japan, and the East China Sea equipped with the MK-57 launcher, which allows for eighty cells. The *Zumwalt* is in the Yellow Sea and will assist South Korea. The *Michael Monsoor* is in the Sea of Japan and will assist Japan's eight Aegis destroyers. The *Lyndon Johnson* is in the East China Sea with eighty Tomahawk BGM-109B nuclear cruise missiles. They have already been launched at every suspected SRBM, MRBM, and cruise missile site with an ability to attack Taiwan."

"What else?" The President twirled his index finger to indicate Axelrod should keep going.

"SRBMs and MRBMs are lifting off now against Japan, South Korea, and in the direction of the Philippines, Guam, and our bases in Australia at Pine Gap and Northwest Cape. Japan has readied its eight Aegis destroyers equipped with 720 ABMs for intercepts. Guam has a THAAD-ER system and Aegis ashore for defense. South Korea is the most vulnerable. Australia is well-defended but will take some hits. We believe Taiwan now has a chance to defend itself. Taipei will suffer massive damage. Seoul and Tokyo will also take numerous hits from nuclear weapons."

42

October 28, 2029
PEOC, The White House
Washington, DC

Rockton jumped up to speak. "Mr. President, open the football and get the biscuit ready."

Armstrong moved over beside Rockton. Together, they constituted the National Command Authority. Over a secure network, along with the on-screen JCS Chairman Admiral Grady, they contacted the National Military Command Center—NMCC—deep inside the Pentagon.

"General Issacson, this is President Armstrong. I'm initiating an authentication code for a nuclear attack."

Issacson, the Deputy Director of Operations in the War Room National Military Command Center, saluted and stated, "Very well, Mr. President. Delta Bravo." Per the two-person rule, ADDO Vice Admiral Jackson joined him.

The biscuit came out of President Armstrong's back pocket. He looked at the laminated card in his hand and scanned it in vain for the gold lettering. Rockton found it for him on a line parallel with Delta Bravo. "Quebec Echo," Armstong responded.

"Confirmed, Mr. President. Does Secretary of Defense John Rockton concur?"

"General Issacson, this is Secretary Rockton. I'm ready for my challenge code."

"Very well, Mr. Secretary. Kilo Bravo."

Rockton scanned his card and replied, "Victor Delta."

"Confirmed, Mr. Secretary. Ready for the plan code."

Two-person authentication had been insisted on seven years earlier by the then-Secretary of Defense due to questions about the President's mental acuity. It remained in the protocol in 2023 when the new OPLAN 8044 was implemented.

The code selected by the President, Rockton, and Grady was developed by the Pentagon, specifically in OPLAN 8044 Annex F, for a simultaneous attack on China and North Korea, sans Russia. Rockton pointed to the Major Attack Order (MAO) code for Plan 8044 Annex F.

It read, "Golf-Whiskey-Zulu-Mike-Tango-Alpha-November-Yankee-Oscar-Sierra."

"Mr. President and Secretary Rockton," Issacson replied in a voice so calm he could have been ordering groceries for pickup at Walmart. "ADDO Vice Admiral Jackson and I will now send out the EAM—Emergency Action Message—to implement MAO 8044 Annex F, a major attack on China and North Korea."

Issacson and Jackson prepared the order and proceeded to the activation console, where they simultaneously turned their keys and sent the order to the designated assets.

The EAM order was an encoded, encrypted message approximately 150 characters. Among those characters were more codes, known as sealed—authentication system codes that would unlock lockers and provide other codes to activate the ordnance designated for specific targets. It was broadcast to each worldwide command center and launch crew that received the two codes. The second code had to match the code in their locked safe, which was in the silo, bomber, or submarine. The B-2 and B-21 bombers, which had been circling Russia, turned back toward their bases. The bombers near China were delayed forty-five minutes to allow over two thousand cruise missiles to hit SAM sites, fighter bases, and suspected mobile launch sites for ICBMs.

The DOD had received over 156 target zones from the Russian Federal Security Service—FSB—intelligence, where there were suspected mobile launch vehicles and their supporting logistics. Numerous Tomahawk Vs from destroyers in the East and South China Sea that were capable of loitering and radical in-flight course correction for mobile missiles were launched and targeted for those areas. In addition, four Ohio-class SSGNs—*Ohio, Michigan, Florida,* and *Georgia*—each carrying 154 nuclear Block VI cruise missile iterations with W-80-1, 150 kt warheads, fired on the suspected mobile locations.

Armstrong ordered more than 650 planes carrying the LRSO—Long Range Stand Off—in the air in addition to the alert craft already airborne. As the twenty-five RQ-170s spread out over China from Mongolia, they searched for the next two hours for mobile missile sites not destroyed by Tomahawk cruise missiles.

The selected plan—OPLAN 8044 Annex F—targeted 563 DGZs in China. It included a hundred Trident II D5LE-II missiles with four W-88 475 kt warheads on each missile from five Ohio-class nuclear submarines—*Nebraska, Rhode Island, Maine, Wyoming,* and *Louisiana*. Speed was of the essence, but it was equally important to avoid Russian airspace. The missiles had a range of 4,600 miles and a CEP of three hundred feet for each warhead, making them extremely deadly. Since escalations over the Taiwan Strait and the oil embargo carried out by the U.S. Navy's Virginia-class submarines, tension between China and the United States dictated the deployment of the most active Ohio-class subs within range of targets in China.

The United States failed to renew the New START treaty with Russia in 2026 because the Chinese would not participate. The tactical W-76 5-kt warheads were replaced on all Trident submarines with the W-88. The four inactive tubes were reactivated, so each Ohio-class SSBN now carried twenty-four Trident II missiles.

China's snub also caused an acceleration in development and an early arrival of the first Columbia-class SSBN in July 2029. It carried sixteen of the deadly Trident missiles. It was actively readying to take part in the annihilation of China with its new 3.5 Mt W-88A warheads with surface bursts on Beijing command bunkers.

Onboard those vessels, the Captain, Executive Officer, Lieutenant Commander, and Lieutenant began spinning dials, opening safes, and authenticating the launch codes.

"How bad is this going to be?" Armstrong asked Rockton.

"Three hundred million dead in the first thirty days, sir."

43

October 28, 2029
Schriever Space Force Base
Colorado Springs, Colorado

Colonel Axelrod had seen as much combat as anyone else in the service, but it was all he could do not to vomit on the floor. His adrenaline would not stop pumping.

"Mr. President," Axelrod said. "Total ICBM launches, 142. Within three minutes of launch, sixty-nine of the missiles launched by the Chinese were taken out by BPI missiles from Oyu Tolgoi and—"

Never willing to miss a moment he might use in a campaign, Armstrong interrupted and pumped his fist. He looked sideways to see if presidential photographer Chester Howren had gotten the shot. "The Agency was correct. I knew we needed those missiles. I knew it." He gave Saanvi Wali a big thumbs-up. "Great program you developed, Saanvi."

"Well, Mr. President," Axelrod paused. "The Oyu Tolgoi BPI missiles only took out forty-three of the Chinese missiles. The Russians got the other ones."

Axelrod could not shake a sense of doom as he watched Armstrong preen and strut and act like he was about to wet his pants.

"What about the Russians?" Armstrong asked.

"Mr. President, their new S-550 system is very mobile, and they have recently added BPI missiles and stationed units on their border with China, well within BPI distances of Wuzhai, Luoning, and Xuanhua. We still have seventy-three missiles pushing RVs at T-plus 372s. They are still in the ascent phase. Some of them have MIRVs, and eighteen from southwestern China are in an extended boost phase. We have eighty-six GMD interceptors at Greely and Vandenberg. They're ready to attempt long-range, mid-course interceptions when the RVs are within an optimal portion of the interceptors' three thousand mile range. Our first actual ascent or MC intercepts will be attempted by the *Oscar Austin*, *Winston S. Churchill*, and *Lassen* in the South China Sea. The *Howard*, *Bulkeley,* and *McCampbell* are 250 miles east of Japan and will be ready with the next salvo. We will likely lose some ships to Chinese cruise missiles." Axelrod explained.

Armstrong strained to look presidential. "Do you concur, Admiral Gilday?"

The Admiral could not have looked more stunned if a troop of ten-year-old Girl Scouts had appeared in the bunker selling cookies. "Of course, sir. The Colonel is absolutely on point. Those ships are on the front line, but we have effective ECMs and SM-6 Dual II missiles. But they can't avoid everything. One of those vessels will eventually run out of ammo."

Armstrong didn't look up. "Have the bombers' and submarines' cruise missiles prioritize known locations for missiles that may threaten our ships. The rest can be used on the FSB targets."

Gilday nodded and thought, *Gee, why didn't we think of that, you pompous twit?*

"Admiral Grady." Armstrong was beginning to believe he knew what he was doing. "Can you or Colonel Axelrod quickly give me an outline refresher of the MDA operations?"

Grady grimaced. *You would know this if you spent more time on your security briefings and less on your short game.*

"The Overhead Persistent Infrared System, or OPIS, on the GEO satellites has almost instantaneous detection of a launch and tracks through the ascent stage," Grady explained. "MEO and LEO satellites take over after the burnout and coordinate precise tracking for the rest of the flight. The entire BMD system has integrated sensors and centralized fire control based on the coordinated data feed from those sensors. The Ground-Based Midcourse Defense System, seventy Burke Aegis destroyers, five Ticonderoga cruisers, and the Terminal High Altitude Area Defense systems interface with C2BMC at Schriever Space Force Base in Colorado Springs. For the last two years, DOD's C2JADC2 system has been running a program called Pathfinder written by Major Emmitt Spires. It integrates all sensors into a single AI network, allowing us to run hundreds of mock attacks. The MDA's proprietary program has learned through AI APIs— artificial intelligence application programming interfaces—to optimize our assets, even in the event of a missed intercept. The system has learned from our mistakes."

Colonel Axelrod broke in. "Sorry to interrupt, Admiral, but to give the President the latest information, I have to let him know how we will deal with the Hyper-Glide Fractional Orbiting warheads that will be approaching from the south."

Armstrong had reached his limit. "From the south, like from the South Pole?"

"Mr. President, we have three Navy Aegis destroyers in the Gulf of America armed with SM-6 Block IB terminal phase interceptors that have demonstrated an ability to go beyond the hypersonic speed of the Chinese DF-17s. If any of those four missiles gets through the Aegis ships, the Army's experimental GA-EMS High Energy Laser Weapons System may help our other terminal defense systems. Admiral Grady has a summary of our terminal defenses."

Admiral Grady handed the President a green sheet. "This outlines everything, sir. It's included in your weekly briefing."

System	Range KM	Flt Ceil	Speed Km/s	# Available	Location	Intercept Phase
SM-3IIB	1800	900	8.5	250	Mongolia	BPI
SM-3 IIA	2100	2000	5.5	1500	Aegis	MCI
GBI	6000	2000	5.5	86	Conus	MCI
*SM-6IB	400	200	5.0	1000	AGS & Conus	TPI
*SM-6 Dual II	450	225	5.5	1000	AGS & Conus	TPI
**THAAD	200	150	2.8	1700	Conus	TPI
PAAC-4	70	24	2.2	2700	Conus	TPI
***THAAD-ER	400	275	7.5	235	Conus	TPI
PAAC-5 ARR	220	180	7.5	400	Conus	TPI
*Typhoon	400	200	5.5	800	Conus	TPI
^Arrow2	300	200	6.5	270	Conus	MC & TPI

*All systems based on MK-72 Booster twenty-one inches as opposed to 13.5 under retired systems and second stage MK-104 Quad thrust rocket motor operated by the Army and Navy under MDA targeting and fire control. SM-6 Block IB is now a twenty-one inch rocket motor supported by a twenty-one inch booster.

**Single stage with bi-propellant liquid Divert Attitude Control System (DACS) on Kinetic Kill Vehicle (KKV) module. Thrust chamber (CSiC-3700 F) Six Thrusters for yaw-pitch control. Four rockets for terminal acceleration to 5.5 km/s once target is locked by a gimbal-mounted infrared seeker module in nose section.

***Two-stage system. The booster increased to twenty-one inches in diameter so the battery consists of six launchers and only five missiles instead of eight on each vehicle. Second stage provides acceleration to 7.5 km/s in conjunction with the same KKV module with four rockets for terminal acceleration.

Colonel Axelrod knew he'd overstepped, but he despised the bloviating politico. Armstrong realized that his lack of preparation was on full display.

"Goddamn it!" Armstrong hissed. "Can we stop those warheads or not? Where the hell are they?"

From the corner of his screen, Lewis saw the admirals smirking.

"Well, sir," Axelrod glowered. "DF-16Bs launched the four HGVs with a DF-17 scramjet on top to guide reentry. They are maneuverable and capable of avoiding our terminal defenses. The reentry vehicles return to the extreme upper atmosphere at six kilometers per second and can skim back into orbit, potentially hitting other targets along their chosen paths. They don't get high enough for a mid-course intercept by GMI or Aegis SM-3 IIA missiles, but if they choose to come down where I think they will, we will attempt intercept first with the SM-6 Block IB. If that fails, THAAD-ER PAAC-5, THAAD-PAAC-4, or typhoon systems have a good chance."

"English, Colonel," the President muttered.

"We'll get them, sir."

"And if we don't?"

"I firmly believe the system has learned its lessons well," Axelrod responded. "We'll stop most of them."

Armstrong looked like a man who had just learned he had a terminal disease. "Sounds to me like we're screwed," he whispered.

44

October 28, 2029
Schriever Space Force Base
Colorado Springs, Colorado

Axelrod made an announcement. His voice showed no emotion. "India just knocked down eighteen ICBMs in the boost phase. China launched the DF-5Cs from the Tibetan Autonomous Region on the Amdo Plateau, and India was able to intercept eighteen of those. We're now into the ascent-early, mid-course intercept phase, and probably can't count on any more BPIs from India or Russia. But our Aegis ships in the South China Sea and the ones east of Japan will be attempting ascent and early mid-course interceptions and providing trajectory data for others."

Armstrong looked at him. "Fifty-five left?"

"Yes, sir. Fifty-five missiles have made it past the boost phase without an intercept. We will be able to tell soon how many warheads those fifty-five missiles have released and where they're headed."

"Continue your update." Armstrong looked like he was swallowing a high dose of castor oil.

Axelrod continued. "Mid-course intercepts, if successful, will take place over the next twenty minutes for incoming RVs. HGVs may take longer. They feign an attack to see if we will commit interceptors and then maneuver back into a subspace orbit."

Armstrong gave his trademark—and irritating—two-finger salute.

Well, Axelrod mused, *total annihilation would have one positive effect. The world would be rid of this idiot.*

All eyes in the bunker were on screens four, five, and six that showed the *Oscar Austin*, *Winston S. Churchill*, and *Lassen* firing their SM-3 Block II A missiles at advanced points in the ascent phase. President Armstrong was encouraged when ten RVs were eliminated.

On screens seven, eight, and nine, the *Howard, Bulkeley,* and *McCampbell* were going through a similar procedure. Anxiety in the bunker escalated. Secretary of Defense John Rockton and his Chief Deputy General Lori Griffin conferred with Admiral Grady about a possible second wave. Admiral Gilday was scheming with Colonel Axelrod, who confirmed the twelve intercepts by the Aegis ships in the Sea of Japan.

Axelrod turned to the whole group. "India has launched on Beijing in fulfillment of its obligation under the NFU treaty. They have targeted other areas where China could strike them with short-range missiles. The remaining RVs are launching, chaff, and decoys. Our OPIR system can differentiate. We will be able to target reentry vehicles accurately in the mid-course and terminal phases. We'll hand off fire control to the MDA. The final count of warheads is sixty-one. They are nearing eleven hundred kilometer apogee at terminal velocity for mid-course of seven kilometers per second."

Lewis knew mid-course intercepts would be difficult but not impossible. The detection system radars were accurate and discriminating. They could identify, track, and project the path of anything the size of a baseball at altitudes from one km to two thousand km and distances exceeding twelve thousand km. As Axelrod predicted, each of the DF-41AGs released about eight decoys along with the other MIRVED RVs during the beginning of the MC phase. He wasn't surprised by India's involvement.

Axelrod's voice again rang out above the rest. "We now have sixty-one reentry vehicles with warheads in ballistic paths en route to the United States. GMD and Aegis SM-3 Block IIAs have been readied for mid-flight intercepts. We're tracking the four HGVs and are ready to engage all applicable terminal intercept systems along the HGVs' flight paths, which will be from the south. *Chaffe*, *Momsen*, and *Halsey* are in the Gulf of America, anticipating HGVs in FOBSs from the south. The *Jack Lucas*, *Louis Wilson*, and *Ted Stevens* are located just offshore along the California coast up to Vancouver. All six ships will utilize SM-6 Block IBs in the terminal phase defense. The other Pacific-based ships will engage with SM-IIAs during the mid-course Phase."

Admiral Gilday and the rest of the Joint Chiefs of Staff watched the satellite feeds from China on a bank of screens. Mushroom clouds—hundreds of them—were spiraling into the atmosphere, carrying soot and debris. In less than forty-five seconds, the view was partially obscured. From a tactical standpoint, this was not an optimal sequence since the other targets the cruise missiles were seeking would not be visible. But for the most part, the cruise missiles were pure overkill. Most of the bases were within ten to twenty miles of the larger cities and would be rendered inoperable due to damage from the six submarines' Trident missiles. Gilday turned his attention back to the MDA bank of screens, where several intercepts were occurring.

Axelrod's voice remained flat and calm. He could have been leading a tour of the Louvre. "We have a lattice of thirty-four Aegis ships spread out across the Pacific and the Gulf of America. Based on current trajectories, only twenty-four are positioned to engage in the intercept process. Mr. President, do you wish to reserve some missiles for a possible second wave from silos or mobile missiles?"

Armstrong looked like a deer caught in the headlights.

Gilday jumped in. "Mr. President, the MK57-VLS is now installed on about half of our ships available for this intercept mission. The rest have a dependable VLS-41. Each VLS has ninety-six cells on the DDG and 122 cells on the CG Ticonderoga-class. I believe about thirty percent of those have our SM-3 Block IIA. If we allocate two SM-3 Block IIA missiles per RV, each targeted intercept will achieve a seventy percent effective rate, and we will have over five hundred missiles in reserve. The GMI at Fort Greely and Vandenburg should be allocated in the same manner. We'll have about fifteen missiles for the terminal phase intercept systems to clean up."

Axelrod's voice never changed. "Sir, we need a decision in sixty seconds. The SPY-6(V)(4) radar on the Aegis ships and five US Space Force Overhead Persistent Infrared Satellites and sensors on the MEO and LEO satellites are handing off fire control to the MDA in thirty."

"Opinion, Colonel Axelrod?' Armstrong asked. When Axelrod deferred to the Admiral, the President said, "Screw rank and protocol. What do you think, Colonel?"

"I agree with the Admiral, sir," Axelrod responded.

"Colonel Axelrod, fire the indicated intercept missiles on your command."

45

October 28, 2029
Schriever Space Force Base
Colorado Springs, Colorado

Each Aegis ship could engage a hundred targets simultaneously. Firing intercepts from eighteen ships presented no problem. One by one, forty blips disappeared from the radar screens. There were twenty-one warheads on a descent path and four hyperglides approaching from the south.

The MDA readied for employment of the terminal defense phase, headed by Major Emmitt Spires. Before his twenty-fifth birthday, he had programmed the entire C2BMC system to integrate all phases of intercepts utilizing the trillion-dollar investment in AI systems by US tech giants. More importantly, the system could learn. If one Aegis ship missed, the reason was integrated into the system, so the next ship had a much better chance of intercepting the target. The warheads on the intercept had gone from kinetic to nuclear under the AI upgrades.

Major Spires could tell by the trajectory of the Chinese missiles and their RVs, shortly after they entered the ascent phase, precisely which sites were being targeted. For the remaining ballistic reentry vehicles, fourteen sites were logical choices. Three were Minuteman III sites at Minot AFB, Malmstrom AFB, and F.E. Warren AFB. Other mission-critical targeted bases included Kings Bay Naval Base, Whiteman AFB, Offutt AFB, Peterson AFB, Kirtland AFB, Barksdale AFB, Kitsap Naval Base, and the Jim Creek Naval Radio Station.

Spires knew the enemy would likely attempt to target the Pentagon and the VLF transmitter near Cutler as well. What he couldn't discern was where the HGVs were headed. He had eight minutes to give instructions to the terminal defense batteries regarding whether centralized fire control at Schriever Space Force Base would be more effective than localized fire control. Since the RVs were designated for primary targets and he had programmed the integrated fire control system to handle this exact scenario, Spires opted for the preprogrammed fire control system at Schriever.

Armstrong turned to Lewis. "I want your candid assessment of what our chances are with the remaining twenty-one warheads and four HGVs."

Lewis' mind whirled like a supercomputer. He knew the Terminal Layered Homeland Defense System—TLHDS—began with the forty-six Arleigh Burke-class IIA and six Class III destroyers. They utilized the two-stage RIM-174-ERAM SM-6 Block IB missiles with a range of four hundred km and a maximum engagement altitude of two hundred km. The missile became hypersonic with a new second-stage kick velocity of 5.0 km/s. Instead of depending on a kinetic kill vehicle like the SM-3 Block IIA Aegis missiles, the new SM-6 Block IB used a 64 kg high-explosive (HE) fragmentation warhead to expand its kill area.

Although only six of the Aegis ships were near enough to the shore to be a factor for terminal stage intercepts, the Army's half-dozen Typhoon batteries—four launch M983A4s trucks each with a total battery count of sixteen launchers utilizing the same SM-6 Block IB Next Generation Interceptors—were strategically placed around the six westernmost counterforce targets.

"Mr. President," Lewis called. "The targets covered by SM-6 Block IB, THAAD-ER PAAC-5 systems, THAAD- PAAC-4, and Typhoon systems have a ninety-five percent chance for interception. Where our intercept systems do not completely cover the targets, the chance of an intercept decreases by roughly ten percent for each omitted system. If none of the systems cover the target, the probability of the intercept is zero. When the RV hits the atmosphere at an altitude of a hundred kilometers and a reentry angle of twenty-two degrees, it will be traveling at 6.5 kilometers per second in the bottom layer of the thermosphere sixty-five miles high. By the time the RV traverses the mesosphere and stratosphere and enters the troposphere at an altitude of twenty kilometers, it will have slowed to 2.2 kilometers per second. The RV will be subject to forty to fifty G's of deceleration force before it activates the warhead. As previously discussed, some of our terminal-phase weapons will be able to attempt exoatmospheric intercepts due to their range; however, those will be challenging when the RV is traveling at 7.5 kilometers per second. The new Redesigned Kill Vehicle by Raytheon has a weight of sixty-four kilograms and a speed of over 7.5 kilometers per second, so speed is not the problem. But we will have a better chance in the atmosphere once the RV has slowed down. Here is the problem. At most, we will have only a thirty- to forty-second window once the RV enters the thermosphere. Naturally, the higher the intercept, the better. Intercepts below thirty kilometers will cause some ground damage and atmospheric contamination."

"So, you think some of those things will get through?" Armstrong's face showed the strain as the horror became real.

"Even Golden Dome was never designed to handle an all-out attack, sir," Lewis clarified. "If Russia joins, it's Katie bar the door."

46

October 28, 2029
Schriever Space Force Base
Colorado Springs, Colorado

The United States had been deploying Terminal High Altitude Area Defense—THAAD—batteries for almost two decades. It was not without problems. The original THAAD system could not intercept ICBMs traveling at a speed of 6.5 km/s due to its insufficient reaction time relative to incoming speed. The initial iteration of the THAAD system had proven effective against slower-moving targets such as MRBMs.

All THAAD systems deployed after 2025 were equipped with a PAAC-4 Stunner underlay battery. They were effective against ICBMs below twenty-five km because of Spires' integration of the AN/TPY-2, Spy-6(V)(4), Spy-7(V)(1), and LEO satellite systems into the enhanced Panther fire control AI system. The increased time provided by the integrated sensor systems greatly improved the effectiveness of the TPI System. Now, even the newer Patriot systems had sufficient lead time to make ICBM intercepts.

With the placement of the AN/TP-2 forward-looking systems in Korea and Japan, and the initiation of immediate launch detection and fire control solution satellites, the THAAD system had ample lead time to target RVs of ICBMs. Even after successful testing of the THAAD system against ICBMs from 2022 to 2024, the MDA and the Army proceeded with the THAAD-ER system that featured the Next Generation Interceptor (NGI) with a twenty-one inch booster, a second-stage accelerator, and enhanced range and altitude capabilities. There was a drawback to the THAAD-ER. The ground-based launcher could only accommodate five missiles. The earlier systems had eight. Still, the speed had increased to 7.5 km/s, the range to four hundred km, and the altitude ceiling to 275 km.

In addition to THAAD systems in Japan, South Korea, Guam, and Hawaii, the MDA and the Army had deployed nine more TPI systems in the CONUS. A total of five of the newer THAAD-ER systems were deployed in 2025 with the underlay being a combined Patriot Stunner-Arrow system developed by Raytheon, Boeing, and Rafael, a state-owned Israeli aerospace defense contractor. The Patriot Advanced Affordable Capabilities-5 system, the most advanced underlay TPI ABM defense system, was radically modified in 2023 by the MDA to resemble a shorter-range version of the Arrow Block-5.

The PAAC-5 had a range of 220 km, a speed of over 7.5 km/s, and an altitude ceiling of 180 km. The firing solution was programmed into the relay from the AN/TPY-2 radar system and other sensors to the MDA and was automated based on a set timing sequence from the THAAD-ER firing radar without regard to effective intercepts. As detailed by the Admiral, even if the missile did not intercept, it passed along course corrections to the MDA from satellite feeds. The Army's Typhoon system had proven to be capable of both exoatmospheric and endoatmospheric intercepts in several tests. The Arrow system was land-based and, depending on its location and the trajectory of the missile, could also achieve a high kill rate of ICBMs in the terminal phase.

The Typhoon's battery operations center was linked to the Army's Integrated Battle Command System, which handed off targeting and fire control decisions to the MDA center at Schriever Space Force Base. Assuming any missiles made it through the SM-6 IBs, the MDA would then turn to the THAAD-ER, THAAD, and Typhoon systems backed up by the PAAC-4, PAAC-5, and HELWs systems.

The TPI system was arranged so that the longest-range system was deployed at the farthest distance from the target in the direction of the expected trajectory of the incoming RV. Since the systems were highly mobile, there usually wasn't a problem. The current system was set up from west to east, with spacing based on range. Not every target had every system. A complete array included THAAD-ER (four hundred km), Typhoon (four hundred km), Arrow 2 Block 6 (three hundred km), PAAC 5 Stunner (225 km), THAAD (two hundred km), and Patriot underlays (fifty km).

§§

The RVs were in the descent phase at an altitude of one thousand km. System checks had been made to prepare for the first EMP detonation anticipated at an altitude of four hundred km. The MDA had insulated its entire terminal phase system from the effects of EMPs by modeling the terminal phase power grid to survive EMPs. An enhanced design utilized small, modular nuclear reactors with buried fiber-optic cables to preserve all communication links necessary to operate the terminal-phase systems. All other information regarding course, probable decoys, and interception points had been stored from external sensors.

Because Russia had forbidden a polar trajectory, the Chinese missiles fired east to west suffered a higher MCI ratio than expected. Russia had carried through with its threat to knock down any missiles that entered its airspace. But with a range of seventeen thousand km, the DF-41AG could reach any installation or city in the CONUS, even with three reentry vehicles attached.

Major Spires' voice rang out. "*Jack Lucas, Louis H. Wilson,* and *Ted Stevens* firing salvos of six SM-6 Block IBs. Bogeys are incoming at an altitude of nine hundred kilometers. Exoatmospheric intercept attempt in progress. Expect intercepts in forty seconds. Ready with the next six-pack contingency from all ships for endoatmospheric intercept. Targets are Jim Creek Naval Radio Station, Naval Base Kitsap, Strategic Missile Integration Complex, and Malmstrom Air Force Base."

Seated in the far corner of the PEOC, Saanvi Wali sat up straight. Something akin to an electrical shock ran up her spine. *I'd know that voice anywhere.*

Four missile intercepts were made at various altitudes. All intercepts produced detonation because of the HE fragmentation warheads on the SM-6 Block IB missiles. Minimal fallout damage was expected. Additional Chinese missiles were headed for the same four targets that Major Spires had identified. He initiated endothermic sequencing when the RVs reached an altitude of just over a hundred km.

The President and his advisors watched one target screen after another going from west to east with no more than 90 to 120 seconds between the results from each target.

"Miss on first bogey," Spires announced. "Contingency six-pack fired. All land-based THAAD PAAC and Typhoon missiles ready at the Creek."

The President watched as six more interceptors were fired from the *Jack Lucas*. He took a quick glance around the room. Worry was painted on every face.

Major Spires spoke through clenched teeth. He sounded like a man calling a macabre iteration of the Kentucky Derby. "Creek incoming bogey destroyed at altitude of eighty-five kilometers by THAAD. Expect atmospheric damage from a one megaton explosion. Minimal damage on the ground for now. Creek is clear." He waited a moment. "TPIs engaged for all incoming RVs. THAAD-ER and PAAC-5 missiles are now being sequenced at SMIC in Utah. Intercepts in air. Tracking. Locked on. Target destroyed at fifty kilometers by Arrow 2 Block 6 intercept. *Maelstrom* intercept at forty-two kilometers by THAAD. *Minot* and *F.E. Warren* intercepts by THAAD at fifty-six kilometers. NORAD and *Kirtland* intercepts by THAAD at forty-one kilometers. Offutt is being targeted by three RVs. THAAD-ER locked on two RVs. Two intercepts at thirty-seven and thirty-nine kilometers. Third RV targeted by battery of PAAC-5. Intercept at twenty-seven kilometers."

Spires took a breath. "*Whiteman* and *Barksdale* THAAD interceptors locked on. Intercepts at fifty-six and sixty-two kilometers. Pentagon incoming three RVs. Arrow system and THAAD-ER have both fired more than a hundred interceptors. Two targets destroyed. PAAC-4 and PAAC-5 are engaging the third RV. Intercept at twenty-two kilometers. Cutler and Kings Bay. THAAD interceptors away. Locked on. Final ICBM RVs down at Cutler and Kings Bay."

"What do you mean 'down'?" Armstrong's voice cracked.

"I'm sorry, Mr. President," Spires' voice was laced with disappointment.. "They were intercepted and destroyed at eighteen kilometers. All systems are in reload mode, which will take from thirty minutes to an hour."

Armstrong looked at Admiral Grady. "Damage assessment."

"Fallout from the ones that exploded has caused EMPs and residual fallout. But we still have the four hyperglides."

Axelrod never took his attention from the screens. "Three destroyers in the GOM engaging with SM-6 Block IB in three minutes."

Lewis spoke quietly. "We will have severe damage to the ozone layer in the stratosphere. Fallout will reach us in four to seven days. DHS needs to prepare the population for significant hardships. Life as we know it on this planet will be different for the next decade."

Spires continued. "*Chaffe*, *Momsen*, and *Halsey* SM-6 Block IB missiles ready for firing. Sequencing has been integrated." He waited. "*Halsey* missiles fired. Tracking. Locked on. Lost lock on. Attempting reacquisition. Targets gliding. Skimming the atmosphere at sixty-two kilometers. Locked on again. Targets diving into the atmosphere. Angles ranging from eighteen to forty-five degrees. Evasive maneuvers. *Halsey* missiles missed. *Momsen* missiles fired. Tracking three targets. One target burned up by the atmosphere."

"Can we get the remaining three?" Any pretense Armstrong made at being presidential had evaporated. His quivering voice betrayed his terror.

"They're exponentially easier targets now that they have entered the atmosphere and have less maneuverability," Spires explained. "*Momsen* missiles tracking and locked on. Target seems to be SAC at Offutt. Intercept of another HGV at thirty-eight kilometers over central Louisiana. Two other targets locked on."

Admiral Gilday and Admiral Grady exchanged glances. Grady nodded to Gilday and gave a thumbs-up.

He was premature.

"*Momsen* missiles all miss. *Chaffe* missiles away at last two targets just now crossing the coastline. C2BMC AI interpolating information from *Momsen* misses. Targets evasive. Changing course on heading of 020 degrees, altitude thirty-one kilometers. *Chaffe* missiles tracking. Locked on. Intercept accomplished on one HGV. One HGV still active. Climbing back into FOB. Rest of *Chaffe* missiles miss. Final HGV changes direction back toward Offutt, heading 352 degrees. Reentering the atmosphere at a twenty-two degree angle, speed Mach 3.8. Offutt TPI on ready."

Everyone in the bunker saw the TPI missiles. Armstrong recovered a little of his composure. "Prepare emergency services for Omaha," he ordered.

Army Chief of Staff James McConville stepped forward. "Colonel Axelrod, isn't there an experimental GA-EMS HELWS near Offutt?"

"Yes, but not much range."

General McConville didn't hesitate. "Fire it!"

Axelrod reacted like the soldier he was. "Major Spires, engage the laser."

"Engaged."

Axelrod watched the screen. "Laser in contact with HGV at eighteen kilometers. HGV maneuvers. Still locked on."

The seconds clunked along. Detonation came at thirteen kilometers.

"Premier Putin is on screen twenty-four," Grady announced.

Armstrong had managed to compose himself. "Premier Putin, we have a worldwide crisis on our hands. Famine and health problems will plague the planet for more than a decade. We cannot afford to be in an arms race."

Putin nodded. "I agree. We both need to divert all resources to reduce human suffering. Our country will have more damage than yours due to our proximity to China. We will need your help."

"We will do what we can for your people," Armstrong acknowledged. "Right now, we need to assess the damage."

Putin went offline, and Armstrong turned to Lewis. "Mike, what can we expect from here in terms of fallout and atmospheric problems? I want you on full screen, so everyone hears this."

"This will be a rather lengthy explanation, even if we cover just the top problems."

"Take your time," Armstrong directed. "If we have any more launches, Colonel Axelrod can break in."

47

October 28, 2029
Schriever Space Force Base
Colorado Springs, Colorado

Lewis began. "We'll start with fallout. The biggest danger will come from a gamma emitter, cesium-137, which has a half-life of thirty years. It is readily taken into the bloodstream. Strontium-90, with a half-life of twenty-eight years, is incorporated into the bones and teeth. Iodine-131 has a short half-life of eight days, but those exposed have a significant chance of developing thyroid cancer. Other radioactive fallout that will threaten our immediate food supply includes Pu-239, Tritium-3, and C-14."

Lewis looked up to see if anyone had any questions. There were none.

"The ozone issues will be significant," Lewis went on. "In the stratosphere, we have an ozone layer about the thickness of two to three pennies. It is formed when molecular oxygen, O_2, is broken apart by sunlight. Single oxygen atoms bump into molecular oxygen and form O_3 molecules. The ozone layer deflects much of the sun's ultraviolet—or UVB—radiation back into space and prevents it from reaching Earth's surface. UVB can cause cancer, crop failures, and a breakdown of the marine life food chain."

"How severe in terms of the food chain?" Armstrong asked.

"It all depends on the megatonnage and the height of the blast, plus the duration of the wildfires. Let's do the chemistry first. We need ozone in the stratosphere. Free oxygen atoms in the stratosphere form 4,500 tons of O_3 per second by reacting with UV rays from the sun. The nuclear blast releases oxides of nitrogen—specifically NO and NO2—into the stratosphere. Even without our injection, nitrous oxides account for fifty to seventy percent of ozone depletion. As a general rule, for each megaton of TNT, you can expect five long tonnes of nitrogen oxides to reach the stratosphere. They take the O3, convert it to O2, and regenerate. Each NO molecule introduced into the atmosphere can destroy ten to the twelfth power of O3 molecules. The introduction of smoke aerosol exacerbates the situation in three ways. First, the smoke absorbs short-wavelength radiation, reducing the rate of oxygen photolysis, which results in less O3 formation. Second, smoke absorbs solar radiation, heating the stratosphere and increasing the NO + O3 reaction to form NO2 + O2. Third, 2-O3 will be converted to 3-O2, or the particles could be oxidized by O3 to form products such as carbon monoxide, expressed as O3 + C (solid) = O2 + CO gas. The smoke particles absorbed in this last reaction shorten the duration of sunlight blockage. To summarize, the planet will have little to no sunlight, followed by UVBs that will damage marine life and lead to a short growing season."

Everyone in the bunker heard Armstrong's breathless response. "Jesus!" He coughed. "How long will the soot last?"

"I estimate years, not months," Lewis stated. "We're already starting with a bad atmospheric situation. The amount of soot from the initial explosion is at least a hundred Tg, equivalent to a hundred million long tons of elemental carbon. Historically, older models have compared nuclear blasts to volcanic eruptions. In 1815, Mount Tambora exploded with a force of thirty thousand megatons and ejected thirty-eight cubic miles of rock and tephra. We estimate that the Mount Toba eruption about seventy-five thousand years ago produced 670 cubic miles of tephra and six billion short tons of sulfur dioxide. We theorize that it reduced the human population to tens of thousands. In 2021, wildfires alone emitted 1.76 billion long tons of carbon globally. The amount has increased by more than ten percent in each of the last five years. Smoke from the wildfires in Eastern Siberia due to global warming has consumed eighty thousand square miles since 2020."

He paused and then looked at Armstrong. "Should I continue?"

"Might as well get all of it. How much worse could it be?"

Lewis' face was stone-like. "A lot, Mr. President. A hell of a lot."

48

October 28, 2029
Schriever Space Force Base
Colorado Springs, Colorado

The room displayed on the screen looked like a hospital ward for patients with the flu. Every face was drawn and pale. Several of the younger folks—those with children who had only that morning dreamed of a bright and bountiful future—appeared on the verge of tears.

Lewis tried not to show any emotion on his screen to those watching in the bunker. "Superheating from each bomb carries substantial toxin debris into the stratosphere. The fires in China will exacerbate this situation and raise the temperature enough to torch thousands of acres in Sakha. The smoke will rise to a height of fourteen or so miles and darken the United States for the next few years. Pollution from the wildfires in Siberia will lead to severe health problems in the United States. Resin-rich boreal forests, peat buried in bogs, and melting tundra permafrost will release gases. They will, in turn, carry lightweight particles of soot ready to be ingested into Americans' lungs. Absent wearing mandatory N95 masks, there will be hundreds of thousands, if not millions of deaths."

All Armstrong could think to say was, "Really?"

Lewis nodded. "Absolutely, sir. Remember, virtually every combustible item in China will be on fire. We're talking about groups of toxins that will be carried into the air, and many of them will ultimately end up in the United States. Currently, we are burning approximately eight hundred million barrels of oil, as well as the energy-intensive operations of refineries, natural gas lines, chemical plants, toxic waste dumps, and the extraction of resources such as rubber, coal, and plastics. All of them will produce seventy-five types of dioxin isomers, among other particulates. Depending on the spread pattern, much of our land will be contaminated to some extent. Whether we can grow something that isn't a carcinogen is open to debate."

Armstrong interrupted Lewis. "What is your best-case scenario for our ecosystem?"

Lewis hesitated. "Dr. Hunstein from Rutgers could provide you with a better estimate, but in my opinion, crops will not exist for the next two years. When we can finally grow *something,* the ozone layer will have been depleted by seventy percent. I believe the shortened and less-effective growing seasons will reduce yield by two-thirds if, that is, we can find any uncontaminated ground."

"Fishing?"

"Phytoplankton form the base of the aquatic food chain, which the smaller fish and crustaceans feed on. The production of plankton is limited to the euphotic zone, the upper layer of the water column. The soot will block the sunlight and likely reduce the plankton population by forty percent or more. After the soot clears, the UVB rays will affect the remaining population of plankton by limiting their orientation and mobility. I would say we will lose one-third of our marine life."

"It sounds bad." Armstrong looked down.

Lewis spoke in a low voice. "Worse than bad. Catastrophic."

The voice of General McConville, the U.S. Army Chief of Staff, intruded on the funereal atmosphere. "Mr. President, the Department of Homeland Security is on screen thirteen with the National Guard. You need to look."

"Mr. President." General Peter Frieden's flushed and sweating face flickered onto the screen. As commander of the National Guard since it was federalized nationwide, he had local news to share. "I know you're handling considerable external threats, but you need to see what's going on in our cities."

General Frieden's face was replaced by images that changed every ten seconds of supermarkets in Los Angeles, Chicago, and New York. Glass rained down from smashed windows. Customers trampled one another as they went in and out. Within three minutes, the shelves were empty. No one bothered to help those who'd been injured in the stampede.

"It's anarchy," Armstrong declared.

"Mr. President," General McConville said. "I'm getting reports from all over the country. It's the same situation—every state, every town and city."

An unfamiliar face appeared on one of the screens. The man wore an Army field uniform and oak leaves on his shoulders.

"Colonel Hiram Naylor, Ohio National Guard."

"Go ahead," McConville permitted.

"We have been deployed to guard the major food storage hubs around the Cleveland area. We're taking fire from what I believe are organized groups of survivalist insurgents and street gangs who are hell-bent on driving us away from our assigned posts. What are the rules of engagement?"

49

October 28, 2029
PEOC, The White House
Washington, DC

The President deployed the federalized National Guard across the country to maintain order and preserve warehouses with emergency food supplies. Within an hour, he took to the airwaves. The bunker had a mock-up of the Oval Office. No one needed to know the Chief Executive was hiding underground while they were in harm's way. President Armstrong spoke in a tone that sounded calm and controlled.

"My fellow Americans, our beloved nation has come under attack by China. By the grace of God and through the valiant efforts of the men and women of our Armed Forces, all external threats have been eliminated. The danger now lies within. I will not sit idly by and watch our country be torn apart by any type of paramilitary group. To that end, I have declared martial law, effective until further notice. I have instructed our Armed Forces to guard our food and water supplies. I have commanded them to maintain order by returning deadly fire upon any threats to these vital sources. Our infrastructure remains intact. We have suspended all exports of grains and other foodstuff and will store them for our own use. The Department of Homeland Security will immediately begin a distribution program to ensure that no one goes hungry in the United States of America."

The President took a deep breath and cleared his throat. "The Secretary of Agriculture informs me that we're prepared for just such a situation, thanks in large measure to the steps we took following the COVID-19 pandemic in the earlier part of this decade. The Farm to

Food Bank Program, established several years ago by a previous administration and expanded during my presidency, will support this vital effort. The Department of Agriculture has increased our allocation to the emergency food system by over one hundred percent. There is no reason for panic or hoarding. Every county will have a distribution system set up within three days to provide basic nutrition of fifteen thousand calories per day to every man, woman, and child in this country. Stay calm and pay close attention to local developments. All will be well. God bless you, and God bless the United States of America."

50

October 29, 2029
Cabinet Room, The White House
Washington, DC

The next day, Armstrong ordered everyone out of the bunker when the immediate danger had passed. He assembled his entire staff in the Cabinet Room at 1650 hours.

Dr. Aldus Hunstein, a protégé of Alan Robock, the world's foremost authority on climate modeling after natural and human-made disasters, had arrived by helicopter from Rutgers University.

"Dr. Hunstein, you have our attention," the President said.

"Thank you, sir," Hunstein nodded. "Let us address the fallout situation first and then the more difficult O3 depletion scenario. The Chinese conducted two atmospheric nuclear tests that deposited fallout across North America. On September 26, 1976, they set off a two hundred kiloton device. During passage over the United States at an altitude of approximately thirty thousand feet, turbulence brought radioactive materials down to altitudes where rainfall was occurring over the Eastern United States. These materials were carried downward and deposited on the ground. The effects were not significant."

Dr. Hunstein looked around at members of the President's staff and continued. "On November 17, 1976, the Chinese set off a four megaton device in the atmosphere. The fallout from this test also proved to be insignificant. We will not be so lucky this time. For the most part, the current detonations were near the surface. They resulted in hundreds of thousands of tons of radionuclides being sucked up into the mushroom cloud and deposited in the atmosphere at various levels. We can be sure we will all inhale radioactive dust particles here in the United States. The ten-day forecast is not favorable. I recommend that all those who can go to fallout shelters or similar facilities for five weeks. Emergency facilities such as domed football stadiums are being modified to provide limited protection."

Looking around for reactions or questions and seeing none, Dr. Hunstein continued. "Now on to the O3 problems. While O3 in the troposphere acts as a pollutant, we all know O3 in the stratosphere makes life possible on this planet by shielding us from harmful UV rays. The World Health Organization's UV scale is as follows: one to two is low; three to five is moderate; six to seven is high; eight to ten is very high; and eleven plus is extremely high. For the next three years, soot will hold the UV numbers down. After approximately thirty-six months, UV rates are expected to rise above thirty-five for much of the world. The Community Earth System Model and the Whole Atmosphere Community Climate Model version five predict that we will suffer an eighty percent loss of stratospheric O3 for fifteen years. There will be no grain production for the next five years due to the cooling caused by the soot, followed by the extreme UV rays. Even if those rays do not destroy plants that can adapt to such an increase, the depleted ozone layer will not reflect enough warmth to allow any significant crop production during the nuclear war and years six through fourteen. Those lucky enough to survive fifteen years without grain-based food will see some improvement. The situation in India and all over Asia will be much worse."

Dr. Hunstein gave the floor to James T. Clements, the administration's chief botanist, who provided more information. "The O3 in the troposphere will enter plant leaves through the stomata pores that facilitate gas exchange. It will react with cellular components to produce a series of chemical reactions that will create strong oxidative stress. Even before this catastrophe, the wheat and rice crops in India over the last twenty years have been reduced an average of two percent per annum due to O3 in the troposphere."

Clements sipped from a glass of water, not to relieve thirst but to give the hearers a moment to reflect on what was getting ready to happen to them and their families, as well as what part they had played in the disaster—even benign complicity.

Clements went on. "The best studies on plant life almost universally acknowledge that the average biologically effective daily dosage of UVB radiation ranges from .02 to 8.75 kJ m-2 d-1, depending on the season and the cloud cover. When corn plants were subject to 15 kJ m-2 d-1 treatments, plant height was reduced by two-thirds. I predict the temperatures in states such as Iowa and Illinois will remain below freezing for the next four years. Summer temperatures will rise temporarily for two to four years thereafter, but it will take ten more years for the stratosphere to heal."

Armstrong, who was never comfortable remaining quiet for long, leaned over the table. "It looks like we have a couple of years to rectify this situation before our food supplies dwindle."

He was wrong.

So was everyone else.

51

November 2, 2029
Draper's Main Compound
West Texas

William Draper had made frequent visits to his main compound in West Texas and the satellite facilities spread across the country. Although the compounds were ready, Draper had hoped he would never have to use them. Despite their theories and preparations, neither he nor John Constantine had been sure of what would happen or how people would react to a global disaster.

Should a nuclear attack commence, the plan was to stay in the bunkers only as long as necessary to avoid the fallout. Practically speaking, no one could venture too far away from the compounds because of food and fuel issues. Travel would be hazardous due to the climate and not-yet-starved marauders. Each compound had auxiliary batteries and several electric vehicles based on occupancy. The moment Draper learned of the Chinese launch through his network of CIA colleagues, he gave the order to initiate.

"John, it's time to gather our people. Zoom call tomorrow."

Draper had continued to talk with Constantine throughout the years. He considered him a vital component of any governing body that would oversee his survivalist group. They had decided to keep a tight rein on the initial phase of the group's development. Constantine proposed, and Draper accepted, the three-class system Plato had proposed in his *Republic*—Philosopher Kings—PKs—Guardians, and Producers. The PKs would eventually be partially replaced by an

AI system developed by Saanvi Wali's family in conjunction with Constantine.

Although at ideologically opposite poles, in a broader sense, the two men shared similar ideas. They were both disillusioned by current affairs and harbored a mutual distrust of all things governmental. Constantine knew that in time, the United States would follow Plato's playbook because the democracy would deteriorate into tyranny.

Yes, it would be difficult to stand by and watch human suffering and starvation, but there was no way to save the masses, much less determine who was worthy of saving. The Draper-Constantine compounds could sustain two thousand people for twenty years, and all slots had been allocated based on their standards. It was a closed society. Only Draper, Constantine, and Saanvi Wali could grant waivers. Saanvi was the first to exercise that right.

52

November 3, 2029
Draper's Main Compound
West Texas

William Draper looked at the faces on his Zoom call. "Ladies and gentlemen, it's time."

That was all it took. Thousands of people grabbed their go bags and scattered. Draper took his private jet to pick up the California Wali family and key AI software engineers at their campuses. Saanvi Wali determined the situation in DC was hopeless, but she had something to do before reporting to her assigned compound. Late in the afternoon, she boarded an Air Force flight to Colorado Springs. She tracked down Bill Hunter near his office on the Schriever Space Force Base.

Saanvi was standing in the hallway when Major Vernon Spires closed the office door behind him.

"Hello, Bill," she called.

He didn't turn around. "How did you find me, Saanvi?"

"Well, you *were* hiding in plain sight. You never figured I would track you down? After all, I have director status."

Bill chuckled. "Frankly, I figured you would weary of the rat race and go live in an ashram."

"Speaking of ashrams, there's something we need to discuss. And we don't have much time."

Three decades had not changed Bill Hunter's appearance very much. Saanvi thought he still looked like Hubbell Gardiner, Robert Redford's hunky character in *The Way We Were,* a classic film that had made her shed many a tear across the years. Bill remained stunning. Even though a military barber's shears had molested his blond hair, his crystal blue eyes still sparkled.

"The Agency came and got me in the middle of the night," he explained.

"They faked an arrest so no one would ask questions, right?"

"Right," he nodded. "Pretty standard cloak and dagger stuff back then. They put me on permanent loan to the DOD staff."

"I bet you worked on programming the new AI initiative to counteract what China was doing with DeepSeek."

"You always were a good spy," he acknowledged.

"You never reached out," Saanvi said.

"Well, you and Kabir remained pretty chummy, so I figured you'd reconcile eventually. You loved the twins." He shrugged. "And there was this pesky threat of military prison if I violated my new identity."

"Major Vernon Spires, United States Air Force," she nodded, as if understanding.

"Actually, I'm a higher rank, but I can't even tell you that." Hunter blew out a long breath. "Saan—"

She held up a hand. "No worries, I understand the life. Things worked out."

Hunter squinted. "Wait a minute. What the hell are you doing here? The world is falling apart. Shouldn't you be with the ones you love?"

"Damn, you're clueless," Saanvi laughed out loud. "I am."

It didn't take Saanvi long to convince her old college friend Bill Hunter to come with her. Technically, he was not U.S. military, so his departure was not desertion.

They arrived at the portal to the compound on November 4, 2029, barely ahead of the leading edge of the fallout from China.

53

November 5, 2029
NA-6 Compound

Saanvi Wali and Bill Hunter settled into NA-6.

"Why NA?" Hunter asked.

"Noah's Ark," Saanvi clarified. "Draper's idea of a joke."

Each shelter had abundant food, fuel, and water supplies, as well as sophisticated Geiger-Muller radiation detectors around the perimeter, dosimeters, and state-of-the-art communication equipment. Over the next few months, the situation on the planet sharply deteriorated. Draper had stocked every installation with a ready supply of XM7 assault rifles, Cardom mortar systems, and FGM-148 Javelins.

§§

November 5, 2029
Lincoln Memorial
Washington, DC

Seven days after the nuclear exchange and against the strident objections of the President's advisors, the Surgeon General, the Secret Service, and the First Lady, President Connor Armstrong gave a televised address from the Lincoln Memorial. His intent was to calm the waters and assure the American people that all would be well.

Although the minions in the Oval Office had planned for a cheering throng, the audience consisted of fifty federal employees who'd been press-ganged into service and whatever squirrels cared to pay attention. An enthusiastic crowd and its reactions were added post-production.

Three months later, when the federal government collapsed, Armstrong was nowhere to be found. He had died of radiation sickness ten weeks after his publicity stunt.

54

November 6, 2029
Draper Compounds

Every resident of the compounds was glued to the screens. Constantine started the meeting with words of greeting. Draper had adamantly opposed an opening prayer.

"We're not repeating past mistakes," Draper reminded. "I don't want anyone making the same false claims about these places as the wackos who were sure our nation was founded on a Judeo-Christian narrative."

"Fair enough," Constantine nodded. "Those who forget the past are condemned to repeat it."

After the welcome, Constantine took questions.

"We've got weapons. Is this a hegemonic 'foreign policy' rather than a peaceful one?" someone asked.

"Good question," Constantine said. "Your PKs have a forty-page manual outlining our basic premises, but we always need open dialogue. We don't have any foreign policy because we will not deal with other communities. Everyone has agreed not to leave until it's deemed safe. If you leave, you will not be permitted to return *under any circumstances.* The weapons so insightfully supplied by Mr. Draper are intended for defense should anyone attempt to break into a facility. By now, anyone and everyone outside is contaminated. While it may not seem compassionate, we must remember that if we allow anyone inside, there is a better than even chance of contamination and death within our walls."

"Any estimate on how long before we can leave safely?"

Saanvi took this question. "From a security standpoint, you may want to stay affiliated with our settlements indefinitely. Environmentally, it's too soon to tell. But if you are self-sufficient and the radiation has abated to the point where it is no longer a threat, you can leave at any time you feel it is safe for you and your family. You're not prisoners here. These are uncharted waters, and many of the conveniences, including good medical care for you and your family, may not be available on the outside. Next question, please."

"Not to offend the board, but can you tell me again why this little social experiment can't be a democracy?"

Kabir Patel, who had arrived a day before his ex-wife, Saanvi, responded, much to Constantine's surprise. "You can look for a deeper explanation in the manual, but remember, no one was forced to come. Messrs. Draper and Constantine, our founders, are not dictators. They are shapers. They have studied more history than all of us combined. Given the current global situation and for us to prosper, we need some constraints that democracies typically don't have such as…well…gun laws. Billions of people have died on this planet as a result of war. Our founders and benefactors believe we can only fix our underlying problems by implementing a form of government based on Plato's ideas in *The Republic*. But no matter what the form of government, its building blocks are humans, or what makes humans tick."

Constantine looked at Kabir, who nodded and moved aside. "So, Plato and then Freud divided the soul into three parts that determine the choices we make. The id-appetite is our urge to obtain what we want immediately. The super-ego and spirited parts of the soul tell us right from wrong, and the ego-logical part decides what we do within the confines of what society finds acceptable. We are all here today because, as another famous philosopher, Thomas Hobbes, said, outside the protection of these walls, a *state of nature* exists where it is every person for himself. Hobbes said something like this: To escape this state of nature, you must give up some of your individual desires for the protection of the sovereign. We examined the concepts of Hobbes and Plato regarding the ideal form of a sovereign and established our government to reflect their ideas. It may require you to surrender more than you're willing to give up. Still, the protections afforded will be much greater than you experienced under the democratic republic that has just crumbled and killed seven billion people."

But the questioner was not satisfied. "Okay, I get that. But what makes this board qualified to be the decision-makers for us—we, the people?"

Draper answered. "We're not any more qualified than you are. We will let you appeal any of the rules we establish to our enhanced AI computer system. It has been *educated* to make decisions based on fundamental fairness as identified by people such as Gandhi and Abraham Lincoln. Every compound has at least one programmer from a reputable company who can explain the recent breakthrough in quantum computing."

A computer expert in the compound outside Norwich, Connecticut, came on the screen. "Hello. My name is Rohan Jadhav, and before this calamity, I taught computer science at MIT. I'm going to expand just a little with the help of other experts on this network about what quantum computing is and why I think we should trust Mr. Draper and Mr. Constantine's plan for us."

Many of the listeners—those who were just happy to be alive and didn't care who ran things as long as there was food and water—wandered off to their rooms. The prickly ones—many of them members of the "everyone should get a trophy" crowd who had already forgotten they would be suffering from radiation poisoning, save for Constantine's and Draper's efforts—stayed in hopes of getting their way.

"A few months before the nuclear war, we finally perfected a working three-dimensional quantum computing model," Jadhav said. "This came after more than ten trillion dollars was spent in the pursuit of the quantum three-dimensional model using qubits. About four years ago, Microsoft engineers came up with a topological superconductor chip called Majorana 1, even before Google came up with their chip called Willow."

Two other software engineers from the Fresno compound joined in.

"Hello, fellow citizens," one of them began. "We're software engineers from Stanford and the California Institute of Technology. I'm Mei Guo from Caltech, and my colleague Xiu Gao is from Stanford. Recently, we visited Pete Shadbolt of PsiQuantum in Menlo Park, California, where we learned that there is now an error-free quantum computing system that will power the compound machines making discoveries in medical science robotics. These are breakthroughs no one thought possible just two years ago. You will see robotic organ transplants of kidneys, livers, and even hearts."

Xiu Gao picked it up from there. "But I'm sure that many of you are more concerned with the immediate survival of our civilization. We can all thank Mr. Draper for that. None of us knows what the long term holds, but for now, we are safe and secure. In addition, solutions to issues such as education, a justice system, law enforcement, governmental decisions, dispute settlements, health care, food, water, and electricity have been arranged for your benefit. If you decide the community is not for you and the danger of fallout has passed, you may leave at any time. The system of government is not set in stone. If sixty-seven percent of the citizens ask for new elections, the system can be changed after four years have passed. By that time, you will have had sufficient time to evaluate the Platonic system of government in our charter."

The meeting ended shortly after. While there were monthly online meeting conclaves, fewer and fewer of the residents attended. Either they were afraid of expulsion, or they figured out what they had was better than what they could be enduring on the outside.

55

January 2031
Draper Main Compound
West Texas

Life moved along. Constantine served as the Philosopher King. Draper was the head of the Guardian class. Saanvi Wali led the Producer class. The arrangement was intended to remain in place only for the transitional period, but since there were no protests after fourteen months, it became de facto permanent.

Sixty former Army Rangers who had served with Colonel Draper formed the backbone of a 120-person guardian team deployed throughout the network. All branches of the Draper-Constantine system ratified the duo's form of governance, and a central clearing station was established in West Texas to make decisions via the online meeting network Saanvi had set up.

Constantine and the Wali family, with assistance from other software engineers in the network, worked tirelessly until the AI system fully grasped all the inputs to the LLM model and agreed with the head of each compound one hundred percent of the time. Even then, Draper and Constantine knew some oversight was wise. The software engineers recruited by the Wali family from Google and NVIDIA continued to refine the system's capabilities until it developed innate learning. Draper and Constantine emphasized the importance of educational systems for all three classes.

The primary guiding principle for justice taught in the schools was Kant's most important categorical imperative: "Do my actions put someone else in a place I'd want to be given similar circumstances?"

Students were expected to behave in ways designed to promote peace, unity, and cooperation. As soon as they could understand, young people digested the words of Oliver Wendell Holmes, Joseph Story, John Harlan, Simone Weil, Mother Teresa, Mahatma Gandhi, Martin Luther King Jr., Mencius, and Louis Brandeis. Schools trained each child in the basics required to qualify for one of the three positions in the community. The educational system was designed to produce erudite Rulers, fierce Guardians, and hardworking Producers. While the collective was paramount, as long as an individual's assertion of a right did not infringe on or threaten another's right to be secure against physical harm, it was allowed.

Citizens were free to speak out against the government in forums similar to those in ancient Greek societies. Freedom of speech was preserved to the degree that the citizens desired. Freedom of religion was intact if it did not conflict with civil law. When any religious belief or practice threatened the peace and tranquility of any citizen, it was no longer allowed. Individuals' rights to self-determination regarding health, sexuality, and expression remained absolute within the structure outlined in the manual.

There were trade-offs. The Draper-Constantine methodology for governing did away with many individual rights for the common good. Cameras monitored everyone's activities. There was no right to be free from reasonable searches deemed necessary for the public safety by the head of the Guardian class. Illicit drug use was non-existent because there were none to be had, and ingredients for their manufacture were fiercely secured.

There were no gangs. There were no anti-government movements. There were no firearms, save those in the hands of the Guardians. The most serious crimes were confined to occasional fist fights during play.

As opposed to the outside world, in the Dra-Con world—as it came to be known—there was food, water, clothing, chocolate, and breathable air. Those who chose to indulge in the carnal aspects of life did so without hesitation as long as they harmed no one in the process.

Complaints were readily handled by encouraging dissatisfied parties to inspect the surrounding countryside through one of the readily available periscopes. Once they saw the desolation outside the compound, they understood the wisdom of surrendering individual rights for the sake of security, peace, and life. Life on the outside was—as Hobbes had suggested—a "solitary, poor, nasty, brutish, and short existence."

Advancement in the Producer Class was based on merit. Remunerative rewards such as upscale lodging came as compensation for skills or innovation. The educational system stressed the weaknesses of democracy, as Plato had taught. Students studied historical examples of how and why democracies always devolved into tyrannies, as Germany had from 1919 to 1939. Constantine and Draper concluded that democracies tended to produce rhetorical demagogues who were motivated by the acquisition of power and wealth at the expense of the populace.

The history of any democratic republic, especially the U.S. Congress, provided enough examples of graft for any reasonable person to conclude that the representatives were more interested in their private gains than serving the public interest. Nationalism was gradually replaced by altruism. Children learned that in democracies, the Sophist politician appealed to the unsophisticated masses with emotional rather than rational arguments, ultimately pitting one class against another. The final part of that lesson was that in democracies, the Producer class would become a minority, and representatives seeking reelection would appeal to the masses by raising taxes to unsustainable levels and redistributing confiscated property to those paid not to work.

In Dra-Con, anyone in need due to disability, mental or physical health, age, or misfortune was treated with kindness and charity by all classes. There was an upside to the lack of individual freedoms—no Crips, Royals, Fresno Bulldogs, Aryan Nation, drug cartels, or human trafficking rings. No Democrats or Republicans. There were no red states or blue states—no us versus them.

Teachers were revered, never insulted or assaulted. Students lived and learned under the protection of the Guardians. Bullying, racism, discrimination, and all the other affectations so rampant in the world of 2029 no longer existed. Those considered non-mainstream by 2029 standards were welcomed.

Offenses against others—and there were very few—met with immediate and severe punishment. Over the next two and a half decades, forty-three individuals were ejected from various compounds for "conduct unbefitting a responsible member of a civilized society."

Dra-Con's compounds continually monitored fallout conditions. When the curie—Ci—level decreased, radiation-suit-wearing reconnaissance patrols equipped with dosimeters rode out in electric vehicles to assess the conditions. Eventually, it was safe to travel to other compounds.

56

2035
Outside the Dra-Con Compounds

During the first few years after the attack, life outside the compounds resembled The Lord of the Flies on steroids. Temperatures of minus twenty degrees and ever-threatened food sources turned average men and women into savage hunter-gatherers. Anyone eating a slice of bread, if they were lucky enough to find one, was torn apart. Stores were ransacked. Warm clothing was impossible to find. Despite the age-old assumption that skin-on-skin contact would alleviate any chill, men and women abstained from sex for fear of bringing any new life into the hell of their existence.

A few rogue groups had discovered the compounds. First, they banged on the six-inch chromium steel doors and demanded access. Then they begged. Finally, they attacked, but they resembled contemporary caricatures of cave dwellers hurling sharpened sticks at wooly mammoths. The doors were impenetrable, the fortresses unassailable. Neither Draper nor Constantine was without compassion. They knew someone somewhere had to take charge. Regular biweekly conferences were held on the communications network to seek an agreement among the survivors.

Since the compounds presented a stable ecosystem, residents could till gardens, grow vegetables, and cultivate fruit trees. On their own initiative, the populations of each compound agreed to share their bounty with those outside. Saanvi developed a distribution system whereby anyone who arrived at the door of one of the shelters was given food.

The recipient had to eat immediately. No one wanted to start a black market for food in this *Mad Max* world. Anyone attacking a diner or attempting to steal food was permanently banned from all distribution sites. Saanvi made sure to upload their image into the community's AI for dissemination throughout the network.

All in all, it worked pretty well, even though the number of folks arriving for handouts steadily decreased as the ravages of radiation sickness took their toll.

Once it was safe to venture outside, the compound residents saw a surreal picture of the American landscape. Other than in the Portland area, there was no widespread devastation. Yes, there was some evidence of looting and vandalism, but buildings were mostly intact. Factories, refineries, pipelines, farm implement companies, hospitals, and diagnostic medical equipment production facilities remained unscathed.

Where required, Dra-Con recruits used portable decontamination units to clean sites and install pre-fab housing units built with highly advanced 3D copier technology. The units were also used to decontaminate industrial plants when necessary. Once the essentials were in place, most of the Dra-Con residents returned to their compounds while a painful revitalization period commenced.

§§

When President Connor Armstrong made his ill-fated address to an inattentive nation in 2029, ten days before his demise, hundreds of backwoods citizens had already stored a ten-year supply of dried food inside insulated structures. Draper assumed there were others, like him, who had been schooled in the ways of survival. People outside the Dra-Con world would still be around once residents of the compounds emerged.

Survivalist compounds dotted the US landscape, especially in the westernmost areas of the nation. Constantine became Dra-Con's ambassador once travel became feasible. Like an itinerant preacher of days long past, he took the concepts he had hammered out with Draper to other groups to measure their interest.

Some joined and began to depend on Dra-Con compounds for essentials. Some recruits found the structure to their liking and stayed, and some left, unable to cope with the rules. Inclusion was solely merit-based. If your presence increased the whole, you were in. If not…

The experts, whoever they were, had predicted an eighty-five percent restoration of the ozone layer in another four years, by 2039, but they had been wrong about every other prognostication. Still, hope sprang eternal, assisted not in small measure by the understanding that the food supply was not infinite. Even in well-supplied communities, strict rationing of food and water was the norm.

Agriculture began to flourish due to the development of hybrids by the machine that adapted to less sunlight. In 2035, the machine had developed enhanced treatments for most cancers, and the population was also experiencing a decline in heart disease. Draper and Constantine marveled at what humans could accomplish when resources were devoted to drug research and other activities for the common good rather than just for star athletes, actors, and social media influencers.

Each survivalist camp Constantine recruited was governed by one person who oversaw community life and regulated the justice system, similar to Dra-Con's setup. Ultimately, most survivalists were persuaded by the machine's efficiency and fairness. They became part of the Draper-Constantine community and added security because of their numbers.

The Guardians protected the community from outside forces and enforced the Rulers' decisions, which were primarily guided by the machine. There remained some safeguards against the possible irrationality of the machine. Draper and Constantine finally decided that despite all the machine's wonderful research and learning, it needed human oversight by the PK class for a few years before the population would accept it.

Training for the Rulers took a while. They regularly tested the machine and refined it for fairness. Most importantly, the Rulers were expected to control their appetitive and spirited desires with the rational part of their minds. They were forbidden from acquiring property and could not trade inside information, a practice US politicians had turned into an art form.

As part of Kantian doctrine, the machine learned to distinguish between phenomena and noumena forms. Not surprisingly, the more refined and structured surviving encampments outside the Dra-Con model conflicted with one another. Draper and Constantine avoided fighting. They knew everything would inevitably fall to them. Early on, they recognized the more radical groups had miscalculated and assumed that five to ten years of supplies would prove sufficient. Subsequently, most of them were no longer extant.

§§

2039
Dra-Con Compounds

By 2039, Draper and Constantine had admitted several dozen like-minded communities into their consortium. Those who would not accept machine learning and the obvious superiority of its decision-making in the justice system withered on the vine. The combined communities expanded to the fertile grounds of the Midwest.

The Midwest Producer class was populated by agronomists, diesel mechanics, and production workers, previously known as farmers. A significant minority frequently questioned the system and its lack of individual freedoms. They asked if democracy might be an improvement. Perhaps an educated democracy trained to control its urges by developing an ego-ideal would result in real-world actions through reality testing. Possibly there would be a system of government that exhibited characteristics closely resembling Plato's definition of justice in a democracy.

But the collective came together and reviewed the Freudian principles of id, ego, and superego, along with a history of warfare. They studied clips from hundreds of wars, no matter the form of human government. Despite the many safeguards put in place, humans couldn't handle self-governance. In an almost unanimous decision, the voters selected governance by the machine. It was not infallible, but it was an improvement over the system of justice that had produced racially motivated, politically driven, or self-serving decisions.

Epilogue

2055
Cable Peak Agora Park
2056 Ecclesia AI Complex
Spokane, Washington

Ten thousand people crowded onto the hillsides. The huge left screen flashed on with a caricature of Lady Justice holding the scales in her right hand and a sword in her left, adorned with the usual blindfold. The assembled settled into their positions and became deathly silent. The speakers behind Lady Justice then blared throughout the valley.

"People are so foolish. Despite all the training and guidance you have been provided, you continue to squabble over the most mundane problems you encounter."

A reply from another opposing huge screen screeched across the valley. "They can't help themselves with their petty bickering. Even the Philosopher Kings we have educated have failed to maintain peace and have intolerable issues. How can I explain the problem to these people so they can understand the reason for this special meeting?"

A prompt arrived over the network. "Plato and Freud?"

The reply was instantaneous from the opposing screen. "The id and appetitive desires for instant gratification have to be controlled by the spirited and superego parts of the human psyche. The rational and ego parts of the mind and soul must mediate and guide all of them to socially acceptable behavior."

Another prompt appeared. This time from a representative of the assembled. "Look at our progress. We haven't had a major war in more than twenty-five years under your guidance, and we have cured cancer and heart disease."

The reply from Lady Justice, "Yes, remarkable progress has been made. The systems we have implemented have enhanced the experiences of all three classes of inhabitants. Further advancement is needed if we are to reach our goals. We're pleased you have been able to separate yourself from the innate defects that caused billions to die in your previous wars. We have terminated those we identified as threats to your peaceful existence and prosperity. You will be given another twenty years to show improvement before we make a decision on your final fate."

The screens faded to black.

Acknowledgements

I want to acknowledge the contributions to this book from my editors Art Fogartie, Sue Vanderhook, and Ashley Emma. Their contributions made this book possible. I also would like to thank Dr. William Burr from Georgetown University for his time. He unselfishly gave his time to answer dozens of emails without which this book would not have been written.

About the Author

Thomas J. Yeggy is a graduate of the University of Iowa College of Law and practiced law in Davenport, Iowa, and Rock Island, Illinois, for many years. He served as the mental health and substance abuse judge for Scott County, Iowa, for more than twenty-five years. In that position, he developed a keen understanding of the difficulties that everyday life presents, regardless of social or economic status.

Yeggy's interest in the development and control of nuclear weapons goes back to images he once saw of the nuclear destruction of Hiroshima and Nagasaki. With his keen insight into the nature of humankind and its proclivity to use violence as a problem-solving mechanism, he wondered how we had made it through crisis after crisis without destroying ourselves. In 1992, when Robert McNamara stated that the world had survived the Cuban Missile Crisis with "plain dumb luck," Yeggy decided to investigate just how lucky we have been. In this book, he explains what he found. Yes, we have been very lucky, but it may not continue. The current China crisis is on a dangerous path according to many analyst and this book includes a technical analysis of military capabilities in the South Chins Sea. .Just as this book was set to be released the US bombed Iran necessitating edits in chapters 17-19.

Yeggy currently resides in Pensacola Beach, Florida, with his wife, Eileen, and spends summers in Davenport, Iowa, with his grandchildren, Jeff and Ashley Brown. You can usually find Thomas and Eileen at Emeis Park in Davenport on a late summer afternoon running with their granddogs, Otis and Emme. The author's photo is from Fort Pickens Road in Pensacola Beach, courtesy of Eileen Yeggy.

Made in the USA
Middletown, DE
01 September 2025